A CHOCOLATE AFFAIR

Sheila Copeland

A CHOCOLATE AFFAIR

sepia

BET Publications, LLC
www.bet.com

SEPIA BOOKS are published by

BET Publications, LLC
c/o BET BOOKS
One BET Plaza
1900 W Place NE
Washington, DC 20018-1211

All Kensington Titles, Imprints, and Distributed Lines are available at special quantity discounts for bulk purchases for sales promotions, premiums, fund-raising, and educational or institutional use. Special book excerpts or customized printings can also be created to fit specific needs. For details, write or phone the office of the Kensington special sales manager: Kensington Publishing Corp., 850 Third Avenue, New York, NY 10022, attn: Special Sales Department, Phone: 1-800-221-2647.

ISBN: 1-58314-234-7

First Printing: October 2001
10 9 8 7 6 5 4 3 2 1

Printed in the United States of America

In memory of my grandmother, Bessie Wiley. For your strength.

This book is also dedicated to all SCD patients.
Life is a gift and yours to take.
Embrace it, live it, love it!

ACKNOWLEDGMENTS

Father, I continually praise You for the gift, the opportunity, and the blessing of sharing it with the world.

My mother, Georgia Copeland, and the Adams and Bowens families.

Lynda Anderson and the Sickle Cell Disease Research Foundation, Marilyn Beaubien, Charlotte Brandon, Erma Byrd, Dr. Thomas Coates, Pastor BAM Crawford, Gabrianna Crawford, LaVelle DeWalt, Henry Holmes, Frances Hunter, Christopher Lee, Rosiland Lee, Michele McCoy, Dr. Raul Mena, Johnny Newman, Iola Noah, Shirley Northern and the Coalition of Black Trade Unions, Linda Smith and FAME Renaissance, La Ronda Sutton, Maurice Taylor, Shanice Wilson and Flex Alexander, and Bill Whitten.

Special thanks to my agent Paul S. Levine, my publisher and friend, Linda Gill-Cater, and my editor, Glenda Howard. You're the best!

And now abide faith, hope, love,
These three, but the greatest of
These is love.

—I Corinthians 13:13

Chapter One

Keisha watched as the movers loaded the last piece of furniture on the truck and slowly closed both front doors when the heavy vehicle roared to a start. Even inside the cold, empty house, she could hear the culprit, stashed with their precious belongings, rip through the quiet neighborhood, heading toward the interstate. When the motor was no longer audible she felt the tears sliding down her cheeks. It was over.

She felt herself gearing up for a good cry when the sound of a ringing phone interrupted her thoughts and she welcomed the intrusion.

"How ya doin', girlfriend?"

"Wonderful." Keisha smiled, happy to hear her best friend Karla's voice. "And crying."

"Girl, everything is going to be just fine. Now don't go drama on me."

"I won't." Keisha laughed, sniffing. She smiled as she fumbled in her bag for a tissue.

Karla always made her laugh. You can't help loving someone who makes you laugh. She wiped the tears from her eyes.

"The movers just took my things. I still can't believe we're leaving."

"I am going to miss you so much." Karla spoke slowly.

"I know." Keisha was crying again. "What am I going to do without you?"

"Now I'm crying, too." Karla wailed. "This is all your fault."

Keisha laughed when she heard Karla blowing her nose. "We're a pair," she managed after they had a good cry.

"You're going to make new friends and you'll be so busy, you won't have time to miss me," Karla continued. "People will be attracted to you because you're kind and genuine and they can trust you."

Keisha sat on the bare hardwood floor and listened intently. "Me?"

"Yes, you. Do you know how special you are?"

Keisha was silent as Karla continued speaking.

"You'll see. You won't have time to be bored or lonely."

"Hmmm." Keisha wanted to savor Karla's words, and file them away in her memory, because whenever Karla said something was going to happen, it happened. She had told Keisha she was pregnant with a girl before she even had the first thought of being with child.

"I know I want to do something special with my life. . . . Sometimes I feel so useless."

"Keisha, you're a wonderful mother and a loving wife. Eric adores you."

"I know, but is it wrong for me to want more?"

"Of course not. Have you spoken to Jade lately?"

"No. She's always out of town working and she hardly ever returns my calls. She must be really busy." Keisha traced a heart with her name and Eric's in the thin layer of dust that had collected on the floor.

"She never calls me either and she's my sister-in-law. I was so excited when she married Sean. Another woman in the family to balance the Ross testosterone."

"It can get out of control. Whenever the twins and Eric are together, they really cut up."

"Those fine brothers are like kryptonite. Trust me, I'm married to one."

"Kyle is one, too." Keisha laughed. "Do you think he'll ever get married?"

"It would take a miracle. He has the women taking numbers and standing in line."

"Do you know what time it is?" Keisha looked at her watch twice to be sure. "I've got to go pick up our girls from school. I'm about to be late on my last day."

"Kyrie is going to miss you guys so much. You're her other mother."

"And we're going to miss all you Rosses, too."

"Kirk is too jealous. Eric and Sean together and he can't be there. He even brought up the subject of us moving last night."

"Girl, stop. He didn't." Keisha tried not to laugh.

"He looked so sad. I thought he was going to cry. I did everything I could to keep from laughing."

Keisha laughed so hard her stomach hurt. "Men. They are such babies."

"That's why God had to give them helpmates."

"To help a brother out," they finished together.

Keisha was still laughing when she dropped her phone in her purse. She walked through the empty rooms, checking windows and doors, still unable to grasp what was happening so quickly.

An offer was signed and sealed within the two last weeks. Things had moved at warp speed ever since. Her life had been turned upside down and she had mixed feelings about this new transition.

Keisha picked up her keys and looked at her first home, emptied of the treasures that made it her own. She had fallen in love with the five-bedroom house in Fort Lee, New Jersey, the moment she saw it. There was an excellent public school for Kendra and she lived only doors away from Karla.

The back of the house faced a small lake. Every weekend in the summer, someone barbecued if they weren't at the Ross family home in Martha's Vineyard. Keisha looked at the lake, now partially frozen over, and imagined it summer when the couples spent long hours talking and laughing after dinner under the gazebo while the girls played on the swings or chased lightning bugs.

She closed and locked the front door for the last time and dropped the key in her favorite Coach bag that she always carried whenever she traveled, which was often. Life in the NBA . . . but it was Eric's job and most definitely a blessing. With his lavish income, the family lived comfortably and well.

She backed her Lexus coupe out of the driveway and headed around the lake toward Kendra's school.

We could be going to the Nuggets or the Jazz. No offense to the Jazz, but who wants to live in Salt Lake City? Do black people even live there? Her Atlanta soul needed flavor.

Children were already spilling out of the school when Keisha arrived. She was picking them up early from aftercare so they could have dinner before their flight.

"Hey, Keisha. Last day, huh?"

She paused to greet the statuesque Celeste, the wife of Eric's teammate. Celeste was a beautiful woman with a copper mane. She had three kids in the school and her daughter, Tiara, was in Kendra's class.

Keisha nodded and looked at her watch.

"We survived, girl. It can be done. But just know, there's no city like New York City."

"Spoken like a true New Yorker." Keisha wanted to make a quick exit. Celeste had given her the 411 on life as a wife on Eric's new team, and she didn't like the report. Just the sight of Celeste made her feel uneasy and she had no desire to get into a conversation with her.

"Mommy." Kendra spotted her as soon as she entered the lounge where little people buzzed like bees. She had inherited her Eric's smiling honey eyes and rich sense of humor. The rest was all Keisha. She was short, curvy, and spirited, even at five.

"Hi, Auntie Key." Nine-year-old Kyrie, whose black, silky braids reached the middle of her back, followed Kendra. If either of the girls had aspirations of playing basketball, it was Kyrie, tall like her dad and uncles, who played for the school.

"I had a surprise good-bye party." Kendra toyed with one of her many braids as she spoke.

"You did?" Keisha tried to sound surprised. Eric had dropped off White Castle burgers and fries right before lunch.

Kendra took out her mother's cell phone. "Daddy." She spoke into the phone and waited for him to respond.

Girlfriend loves her daddy. Keisha smiled as she pulled off. There was nothing that Eric wouldn't do for his favorite girls.

"There's my sweet boo," he replied almost immediately.

"Daddy, thank you for bringing the White Castle burgers for my party."

"What White Castle burgers?"

"Daddy, stop teasing me. I know it was you. I saw your car."

They all laughed when they heard Eric's infectious laughter and Kendra handed her mother the phone.

"You can't fool my daughter. She's too smart. . . . How ya doin', sweetie?"

"I'm okay, just ready to go. How 'bout you?"

"I'm ready. I cried when the movers took our things."

"You did? Why?"

"That was our first house." She felt a lump forming in her throat and tried not to cry again. "It's a girl thang."

"I know, baby. The new house is nice. It just doesn't have a lake."

Keisha opened the door to the hotel suite that had housed the family for the past few days while the movers packed around the clock. She placed an order with room service as Eric, Kirk, and Karla all came in at the same time. They would have an intimate dinner in their suite. The inn was a local favorite for its fabulous cuisine.

"The last supper." Kirk was solemn as he finished his grilled lobster and rice pilaf.

"Oh, don't get dramatic on us." Karla laughed. "And men are always saying we're drama."

Keisha smiled. They had all been kings and queens of drama since the move became official. Leaving their best friends was the hardest part about the move.

"Let's pray." Kirk took his wife's and daughter's hands as the Johnsons stood up and closed the small, tightly knit circle.

The limo to the airport arrived and through hugs and kisses, sprinkled with tears, Karla handed Keisha a gift-wrapped package and a card.

"For your new adventures," Karla told her before they drove away. Kendra waved until their silhouettes faded into the night.

It seemed as if they had been flying forever when the flight finally began its descent through dense clouds. Keisha reached for Eric's hand as the aircraft sailed through an abyss of darkness into an explosion of light. It was celestial . . . the City of the Angels in all of its glory.

Oh, my God. We're really here.

She felt Eric's long fingers squeeze her hand the moment the aircraft touched the ground and she relaxed. He always knew what to do . . . even when he didn't know he was doing it. That was just one of the many reasons she loved him.

She watched him help Kendra with her coat. He could barely contain the smile that graced his handsome face. Eric was excited and rightly so. God had blessed him with the desire of his heart . . . a position with the world-famous Los Angeles Lakers.

Chapter Two

Jade gave her note cards one final glance as the curator from the Smithsonian's American Art Museum introduced her. It was the first time her work was being featured at the prestigious institution and Jade was elated.

She felt a tiny poke inside her abdomen before she had a chance to get nervous. It was as if to say, "You go, Mommy," and she smiled. Jade, five months pregnant and five months newly married, had just started to show.

"It happened while we were on our honeymoon in Exuma, in that house without a phone or a television and you wouldn't let me paint," she had told her husband, Sean, when she realized she was pregnant.

"I did let you paint." He had been delighted with the news.

"You sure did as long as it was on your body. That was some of my best work that never made it on canvas."

"It sure was some of your best work because I still remember every stroke."

She smiled at the thought of her husband's twinkling eyes and electric smile and it made her insides melt like butter. She swallowed hard and forced her mind back into the present and on the curator.

"Ladies and gentlemen, the Smithsonian is pleased to present one of our newest and most fascinating collections of paintings, 'East Meets West—Third World Flavor,' by Ms. Jade Kimura."

She was greeted with a hearty round of applause as she stood behind the podium.

"I'm so honored to share my favorite collection with you today. My work is very personal to me because it is the essence of who I am. My use of acrylic and watercolor combined with Japanese brush techniques gives my Caribbean scenery a unique touch.

"It also speaks of my biracial heritage. My mother, Judith, a dancer, is from Kingston, Jamaica. My father, Paul, a commercial graphic artist, was born in San Francisco to immigrant parents from Osaka. They met and fell in love while attending California Institute of the Arts."

Jade paused briefly to survey the sea of faces representing various nationalities, and smiled. She was no longer an artist embraced solely by the African-American community, but the world.

The silence was deafening as the audience hung on to her words. Jade turned her note cards facedown and spoke from her heart.

"I am proud to be Japanese and Jamaican. You'll find that my paintings reflect the legacy of these two diversely rich cultures. I'll be available for any questions. Thanks for coming."

She sighed with relief as the crowd dispersed in every direction to inspect the vivid paintings lining the walls of the gallery. Captivating colors danced across the canvases, making you swear that you could hear the swell of the sea and feel the rhythm of steel drums.

Jade saw a young black woman making her way through the crowd toward her before she had an opportunity to step away from the podium. It was obvious the woman was anxious to speak with her, and Jade couldn't wait to receive feedback on the collection. She smiled warmly at the woman.

"What's it like being married to Sylk Ross?"

"Excuse me?" Jade wanted to be sure she had heard clearly.

"What's it like being married to Sylk Ross?"

"I'm here to discuss my work, not my husband. Is there anything I can tell you about it?" Jade stared at the woman in disbelief.

"Not really. I love basketball and I wanted to meet Sylk's wife. Will you sign this basketball for my son?"

Jade thought she would lose it when the woman pulled a Sylk Ross basketball out of a shopping bag and thrust it toward her with a pen.

How dare she bring a stupid basketball to the Smithsonian for me to sign!

Jade took the pen, signed her name across the bumpy surface as best she could, and walked off in a huff. She still struggled with the fact that her husband's fame had catapulted her almost overnight into the public eye. She knew Sean had nothing to do with her talent . . . that was God given, but there was no denying that since their marriage she was inundated with speaking engagements, and sales had escalated.

Anyone who was anyone had to have a Jade Kimura. One of the larger originals had gone for over a million dollars at a charity auction. Everyone wanted her originals now, but there was a time when she would have sold one for practically nothing, just for the satisfaction of knowing someone besides her was enjoying it.

"Good evening, Mrs. Ross." She was dead tired when her doorman opened the door of the limo when it pulled into the circular drive at the Marina Bay View Towers. It was one week after her debut in Washington and she was home. Sean had purchased the penthouse in Marina del Rey so his wife could be more accessible to her gallery in Beverly Hills and to UCLA, where she taught a class in water media painting.

Unable to make the long drive to Santa Barbara after a day of work in the city, she would stay in a hotel, and Sean wasn't having it. He understood how important her work was to her and he wanted to be with her, so they had moved to the Marina and stayed at the ranch on weekends.

"You're home." Sean sprang to his feet and opened the door the moment he heard her key in the lock.

"Hi, baby." She gave him a kiss on the lips and when she tried to pull away, he pulled her closer.

"I missed you, baby."

"I'm so sleepy, but if you keep that up you're going to wake me up."

"Those were my intentions." He picked her up, carried her into the bedroom, and began undressing her while her white Maltese, Satin, yapped for attention.

"I can't, sweetie, not tonight. I'm too tired."

She kissed him, scooped up the little dog, placed her in the bed, and climbed in next to her and was asleep in a matter of seconds.

"Eric and Keisha are here." His voice was soft and tender the following morning when she snuggled up next to him. He cuddled her in his long arms and rubbed her stomach while they talked.

"That's nice, baby. You finally got your best friend here."

"God is good. I knew Eric would come to LA when I first moved here. God just had to work out the details. Now my boy is a Los Angeles Laker."

"Want some breakfast, sweetie?" She was not in the mood for basketball first thing in the morning, especially after the incident at the Smithsonian.

"I had Dora make your favorite eggs and sausage to welcome you home." On cue, the couple's Salvadorian housekeeper knocked on the door and entered the bedroom with breakfast.

Jade tried to cook at least twice a week. Sean cooked if he wasn't busy, or they went out to dinner or ordered in from one of the Marina's many fine restaurants. She fed the Maltese a piece of sausage and kissed her on the head.

"Baby, Keisha's been over there by herself trying to settle in. I've taken her around, but she's really looking forward to seeing you."

"Okay, I'll get over there to see her as soon as I can, but I'm really busy right now."

"Make some time for her, please. She's my best friend's wife. Take her out to lunch for me."

"You know I'd do anything for you." Jade put the dog on the floor and locked the bedroom door." Now it's time for me to give you your welcome-home present."

It was a month before the ladies sat down to dinner in Beverly Hills at Reign. Keisha was already seated at a table when Jade arrived twenty minutes later.

"I'm sorry I'm so late, but I had to go over some orders with my assistants. I had to hire a second girl just to do matting. I was at the Smithsonian a month ago and I'm still filling orders. So how are things with you? Sean tells me you guys are living in Ladera Heights."

"I've almost got the house together and I'm going to have you guys over for dinner real soon. This was our first time changing teams since we've been in the NBA."

"I guess that could be a little rough, having to pick up at a moment's notice." Jade flipped open a menu and tried to be interested in Keisha's conversation instead of the work waiting for her at the gallery.

"Eric says some families have to move almost every season. I'm glad we're in a city with friends. Want to come to a game with Kendra and me one night? Karla, Kirk, and Kyrie used to come all the time." Keisha smiled at Jade and finished the rest of her salad.

"I'll try and come but I'm usually extremely busy. I have my gallery to run. I'm always somewhere speaking, and I teach twice a week at UCLA Extension. I haven't held a paintbrush in weeks and I've got all these fabulous ideas running through my head. I hope they stay there until I can get them out."

Jade tossed the menu aside and started munching on the ice in her water glass. "I've been eating ice like crazy the last few months."

"You're just having cravings. I can't believe you're expecting already."

"The baby's due in May. I didn't plan on getting pregnant so soon but we do want a baby. Sean really wanted a girl, but it's a boy." Jade rubbed her stomach as she spoke.

"You've really got a lot on your plate. I thought I had a load with Eric's games and Kendra's schoolwork. I try to go to all the home games and I join him for some of the road trips. He likes for me to be there and I love basketball. Kendra's only five, but she's in first grade. I home-schooled her for kindergarten myself." Keisha smiled, pleased with herself.

"So you're *just* a housewife?"

"A wife and a mother. It's a full-time job."

"I'm a wife and I'm about to become a mother, but I would go crazy if I didn't have my work. I want it all. What did you do before you married Eric?"

"I kept track of budgets and expenses for my father's research. Aren't you going to cut back on your schedule after the baby is born?"

"Just long enough for him to adjust to his nanny." She motioned for a waiter to bring her more ice.

"Nanny? You're going to let someone else raise your child? I could never do that."

"Well, I could never stay home all day with a baby. I'd go crazy." Jade and Keisha stared at each other, amazed by their differing viewpoints until Jade's cell phone interrupted the uncomfortable silence between them.

Saved by the bell.

Jade snapped her phone closed and placed a credit card on the table. "My girls need me back at my gallery." She signed the check and practically ran out of the restaurant.

*　*　*

"We have nothing in common." Jade and Sean were having dinner at the Cheesecake Factory. She looked at her husband as he swirled noodles from his favorite Cajun jambalaya pasta around a fork. "She is so boring and she needs to get a life. Eric said this and Eric said that. Can you believe she home-schooled her daughter?"

Sean had nothing to say but she barely noticed.

"My schedule is crazy enough already. I know you want us to be friends, but I don't have time right now. You understand, don't you, baby?"

Chapter Three

Topaz put on a pair of extra-dark sunglasses, fluffed her hair, and checked her makeup while she wondered if she should give her Mercedes to the valet parking attendant. She looked at the restaurant and made a face.

I am not in the mood for this, especially after dealing with those people all morning. I should have changed this meeting with LaTrell to another day.

She debated calling his office and canceling, while the valet man stood by the car all hunched up in his little jacket from the cold, tapping on the window. It was a chilly evening in late January.

"I need a drink." She grabbed her sable coat from the passenger seat, snatched her bag, and released the door lock.

"I won't be long. Keep it near the front." She heard her cell phone ring as she pulled the golden fur, which matched her hair, around her body and entered the restaurant.

"I'm sorry, but I'm not going to make it, beautiful."

"LaTrell." She sighed as she gazed around the crowded restaurant.

"Sorry, baby, but it couldn't be helped. I'm still in the studio. Order yourself some champagne on me."

"I intend to."

Topaz snapped off the phone and dropped it in her purse. Everyone stared as a waiter led her through the restaurant to a quieter section. As she passed through the tables, two very pretty women, one black and the other of Asian and black descent, caught her eye, and Topaz tried to remember from where she knew the attractive black woman.

It couldn't be her. She paused beside their table for a closer look.

"Keisha?" Topaz removed her dark glasses to be absolutely sure. The woman looked up and screamed and Topaz screamed with her. "Girl, what are you doing here?"

"I live here now." Keisha jumped up and hugged her.

"Really?" She pulled out a chair and looked at the waiter. "And bring us a bottle of Cristal." She stashed her fur and purse on a chair and focused on Keisha.

"So you're living in LA now. Mother mentioned something about you being here but she didn't say you were moving. That's great."

"Eric's playing for the Lakers." Keisha couldn't have been prouder.

"A Laker . . . that's fabulous, Key. How many years have you guys been married now?"

Jade let out a long sigh, pretending to be bored.

"Five years last June. We're working on number six."

The waiter returned with a bottle of champagne and poured each of them a glass.

"To my home girl from Atlanta. Welcome to LA." The ladies clicked glasses and sipped the bubbly.

"I needed this—" Topaz started.

"I went to school in Atlanta. Spelman." Jade cut her off, attempting to get into the conversation.

"You two know each other, right?" Keisha looked at Topaz and then at Jade.

"We've met. I'm Jade Kimura Ross." She extended a hand.

She's Sean's wife. . . . How could I ever forget?

Topaz ignored Jade's extended hand. "I'm sorry, but I don't remember you. I meet so many people." She gave Jade one of her prettiest smiles and Keisha covered her mouth to keep from laughing. She had watched her in operation since kindergarten. Leave it to Topaz to put Ms. Artist in her place.

"Girl, can you believe Gunther has a son?" Topaz finished the champagne in her glass and poured another.

"A son? Get out. By who?" Keisha refilled her glass and was about to pour some of the golden liquid into Jade's flute. "Wait a minute. You're not supposed to be drinking, you're pregnant."

"This little bit won't hurt me." Jade took the bottle and emptied it into her glass. "Go on, Topaz. You were telling us about someone having a son." She sat there sipping her drink waiting for details while Topaz and Keisha exchanged glances.

"Gunther has a son, Keisha. Gunther Lawrence Jr. Just a few weeks younger than Turquoise. His skeletons just keep falling out of the closet."

"How did you find out?" Keisha bit into a coconut-battered shrimp.

"I was trying to be nice and let my daughter spend time with her father's family, Gunther's youngest sister, Rosalyn. I liked her and so did Turquoise, so I would let her go over there once a week and spend the night. One day when I go pick her up, she's playing with the cutest little boy. I asked who he was and Rosalyn starts looking kind of strange. Out walks this beautiful Latina woman named Carmen and she starts talking to the baby and calling him Gunther."

The ladies hung on to her every word.

"I didn't think anything at first until this Carmen tells me Gunther is the father of her baby, too. . . . Excuse me. Can we get another bottle of champagne over here?"

"Go on." Keisha and Jade were practically shouting. A waiter served them more champagne while Topaz grabbed a shrimp and passed the tray to Jade.

"Don't be cute, you know you're hungry. I remember what it was like when I was pregnant. I had to watch my weight." Topaz smiled at Keisha when Jade placed several of the shrimp on her plate.

"Topaz, what happened?" Keisha begged.

"You guys are funny . . . too bad this isn't. So I ask her what she's talking about and she looks at Rosalyn, who tells me it's true that this little boy is Gunther's son. Carmen had to spend some time in jail. She was the skank who cashed all those forged checks for Gunther."

"What?" the girls chorused while Jade placed the remaining shrimp on her plate.

"She was the teller at the bank where Gunther cashed all those forged checks. She claimed she knew nothing about it. But she did. They should have let the skank rot in jail. Rosalyn wants me to give Carmen money for the baby because if Gunther was alive, he would never allow his son to go without. So I told the bitch to sell the car Gunther bought her if she needed money. They could have been trying to run some kind of scam or something."

"That's right." Keisha and Jade agreed.

"So they sued me."

"Who?"

"This Carmen Martinez bitch and Gunther's family. I just left the courthouse. Can you believe it?"

"They sued you? Gunther had a will, right?" Keisha couldn't believe what she was hearing.

"He left everything to me and Turquoise, but they're contesting the will now based on the fact that he never knew about the baby."

"Is it really his?" Jade finished off the last of the shrimp.

"It's his. My attorney had them prove paternity before we went to court. The press was everywhere. I don't have time for this crap. I'm trying to get on with my life. I've got a new album to record. I was supposed to meet my A-and-R guy to discuss material and he canceled. I almost canceled him but I'm so glad I didn't now because I would have missed seeing you, Keisha."

Topaz smiled and the room lit up.

"I can't believe you've been here a month and haven't called me, Keisha."

Jade let out a long sigh, bored again. "Keisha, I'm leaving now. I have to stop by the gallery and then I'm meeting Sean at the apartment."

Topaz looked Jade up and down while Jade collected her things. "You came with *her?*"

"No, I have my car."

"Good." Topaz gave Jade a triumphant grin as if she had won some unspoken battle. "We have a lot of catching up to do."

"I'll call you later, Jade," Keisha called after her as she walked away.

"Don't bother. I'll be having dinner with my husband." Jade didn't even look at the ladies as she left the restaurant.

"What's up with her?" Topaz poured them each another glass of champagne.

"I don't know. We had so much fun in the Bahamas when she and Sean were married, but she doesn't seem like the same person now."

"Maybe it's the pregnancy." Topaz plucked a shrimp from the plate the waiter sat in front of her.

"I don't know what it is. Eric and Sean are counting on us to be best friends like them. After our first dinner, I promised myself never again, but I'm trying. How can I tell my husband I don't like her?" Keisha was really bothered.

"Eric's cool. He'll understand. Here, have some more champagne."

"What he won't understand is me coming home drunk. Girl, you are so bad." Keisha giggled.

"You love it." Topaz laughed. "I am so glad you're living in LA. We can be friends again?"

"Friends again." Keisha smiled warmly.

"Great, I've missed you, Key."

"Me too." The ladies stopped eating to embrace.

"Keisha." Topaz was whispering. "I need to ask you something."

"What is it?" Keisha was surprised to hear the serious tone in her voice.

Topaz glanced around the restaurant and lowered her voice even more. "Have you seen Germain?"

Keisha looked into Topaz's sparkling amber eyes now clouded over with pain, and wanted to cry. It was hard to believe this was the same person who had just entertained them with the latest gossip and turned a boring dinner into a party.

She hoped she would never have to identify with the pain she saw in her friend's face. She couldn't imagine her life without Eric and hoped she would never have to. "You still love him, don't you?"

Topaz could only nod her head in agreement. The tears had collected too quickly and she was afraid to let them fall because they might never stop. She never thought she would fall apart by just mentioning his name, but this was Keisha and she didn't have to pretend with her.

"I think about him all the time. Have you seen him?" Topaz finally managed to ask.

"He's been at a cosmetic surgery conference in Sweden. He'll be home next week." Keisha found a tissue in her bag and handed it to her.

Topaz quickly brushed away a tear. "He won't talk to me. And he won't let me see Chris. But I want him back. I want him back." She was whispering again. "Will you help me?"

Chapter Four

Nina barely noticed the long line of students waiting to register for UCLA Extension classes. It had been a hard decision right up to the end. Between Topaz and Jamil, she didn't know who was worse when it came to putting demands on her time, and they had both hit the ceiling when she told them she was going to school.

She pushed her registration form across the counter to a handsome brother who gave her a "what's up?" smile before he began typing on a computer.

I hope I didn't mess up and miss out on one of my classes by waiting until the last day.

She watched him tap a few more keys and give her another seductive smile. "So you want to be a writer, Ms. Beaubien?"

"Yes, I do. Why do you ask?"

"I just thought a sister as fine as you would be a model or an actress. Do you do videos?"

"No, I don't. Can I have my schedule, please?" She smiled. He smiled back and gave her the admission slips for her classes.

"That feature film class was full but they opened a second one and I put you in that. It meets on the same day as your novel writing class, so now all your classes are on the same day. I get off work right after your last class in case you want to thank a brother properly."

Nina looked at the hand that held on to her fingers and smiled. *Brothers . . . you had to love them for trying every corny line in the book.*

"If you had come up with a line that was even slightly original, I would have considered your offer because you're cute. Maybe next time, my brother, and thanks for hooking a sister up."

He was speechless when Nina winked and pulled her hand away. She was still laughing when she stopped by the cashier and wrote out a check for her tuition. Now it was official. She was finally going to take some writing classes. Every time she had tried before, something always managed to get in the way . . . a tour, a new album, Jamil's label deal. Whatever . . . however . . . it was always about them.

She skipped down the stairs and out of the building, singing until she stopped in front of the shiny, new Range Rover. She was so proud and pleased. She had paid cash for her trophy car and got it for an excellent price. It was barely a week old. She loved the black SUV with camel leather seats for its smooth ride, but most of all she loved the sense of accomplishment. She had made good money working as her cousin's personal assistant, which was one of the reasons it had been so hard to pull away. There was never a dull moment working for Topaz, but her life was never her own. The sun rose and set with her overseeing every detail of the superstar's life. That might float a lot of boats, but it did nothing for Nina. She wanted her own . . . but exactly what she wanted . . . she hadn't figured that out yet.

She stopped at In-and-Out Burger and ordered double cheeseburgers, fries, and chocolate shakes and drove like a madwoman to the studio where she was meeting Jamil.

Are you a model?

She laughed and stuffed a few of the hot, crispy potatoes into her mouth.

Not in this lifetime.

She liked french fries and shakes a little too much for that. Jamil was always teasing her about her booty. He liked a little junk in her trunk. It was one of two qualifications required by every black woman to be a bona fide *sista*. The other was good potato salad. Nina had it going on in both categories.

Jamil was sitting at the mixing board when she arrived at the studio. He spent very little time in his Beverly Hills office. If he wasn't taking some artist to dinner he was in the studio. She handed him the bag of food and sat down next to him. For once they were alone.

"Thanks, babe." He kissed her and took a bite out of the burger. "You must have been reading my mind."

"Where is everyone?"

She looked around the studio expecting one of the boys or some hoochie to pop out any minute. As far as she knew, Jamil was faithful, but that didn't stop the girls that hung around the singers from getting ideas. Nina couldn't blame them . . . Jamil was fine and rich. His boyish good looks and charm always had some honey on the prowl.

"I'm here." He pulled her into his lap and kissed her. "Who were you looking for, Brian McKnight?"

"Is he here?" She jumped up and pretended to look for him.

"Nina." He looked genuinely hurt.

"Aw, boo. You know I only come here to see you." She sat back down and kissed him. "What are you working on?"

"Just a remix." He pushed a button and a nice smooth track flooded the speakers.

"That's not hip-hop." Jamil's signature sound won him producing and writing credits on all the superstars' projects. He had been responsible for Topaz's mega success. "And that's not yours. You didn't write that." She looked him up and down, waiting for some sort of explanation.

"Woman, that is my music. Would you be quiet and just flow?" He pulled her into his arms so they could slow-dance.

"I got my classes," she whispered in his ear.

"Nina. You're ruining the moment here."

"What moment?"

"This is not going the way I planned." He flopped into his chair and cut off the music.

"What? What's wrong, boo?" She sat on his lap and stroked his face.

"Nothing." He kissed her as he reached into his briefcase and took out a velvet ring box and handed it to her. "Here. I was going to sing to you but you wouldn't stop talking."

She stared at the ring box and then at Jamil. "What did you do?"

He took the box and opened it so she could see the five-karat baguette and she gasped. "I love you, Nina, and I want you to be my wifey."

"Your wifey, Jamil?" She looked at the diamond and then at him. "I don't know what to say."

"Yes would be nice."

"Jamil . . . you said you understood."

"You mean about school and stuff and you needing your space?"

"Yes. Then what's up with this ring?"

"That's about me needing you by my side. I've worked hard to get where I am and I'm ready to settle down, get married, have some babies, and travel."

"Travel? The most you travel is from your house to the studio, Jamil. We only spend time together when I come here. You didn't hear anything I said."

"I heard you, baby. And I'm all for your little writing thang, but you can do that on the side. You know I need you to help me with the label. Once that's up and going, we'll take a long vacation and make some pretty little babies."

He kissed her long and hard before she could say another word. The sound of laughter and voices grew louder as one of his groups entered the studio. He closed the ring box and placed it in her hands.

"Jamil . . ."

"Just take the ring, baby. It's yours. We'll work all the details out later." He slapped her on the butt and grinned. "With your fine self."

She slipped out unnoticed while he exchanged pounds with the boys.

She was relieved when she arrived home and saw that Topaz's Benz was missing from her collection of cars. She needed some time to herself to absorb what had just happened.

Despite her declaration of independence from her cousin, she had chosen to remain at the Bel Air house with her. She had the west wing to herself and a Thai cook at her disposal. There was freedom and there was foolishness.

She relaxed in the pink Jacuzzi tub full of swirling scented bubbles, savoring the moment.

Every time I try to do something for myself . . .

"Nina. Nina." She sprang to attention, trying to remember where she was and what day it was. She had fallen asleep. She jumped out of the tub and pulled on a robe, knowing that it would be only a matter of seconds before Topaz and her latest drama invaded her space.

"Nina." Topaz placed the pretty toddler with copper hair and skin and her mother's golden eyes on the floor. She immediately climbed onto the bed next to Nina.

"Hi, Turquoise." Nina kissed the little girl and focused on her cousin.

"Nina, guess who I had dinner with tonight?"

"You said you were meeting LaTrell."

"LaTrell canceled so I ended up having dinner with Keisha."

"Keisha? Who's Keisha?" Topaz didn't have many friends and Nina knew all of them. She had never seen her get all geeked up over a female. Most women couldn't tolerate her because she was so pretty.

24

"Keisha, my home girl from Atlanta. We used to be best friends."

"That Keisha. I thought you couldn't stand her."

"Oh, that's all in the past. We're friends again. She's living in LA now. Her husband, Eric, is playing for the Lakers."

"That's right. He was traded from the Concordes. He used to play with Sylk Ross. Aren't they like best friends or something?"

"Yeah, Keisha was having dinner with his wife, Jade, who is a trip."

"Are you sure you aren't still mad at her because she snagged that fine Sylk Ross?" Nina gave her a wicked grin and waited for a response to the button she had knowingly pressed.

"Please." Topaz picked up her daughter and inspected her diaper. "You know I was never really into him. If I wanted Sean, I could have had him."

She dug in the diaper bag and produced a fresh diaper and baby wipes while Nina started singing "Virgin Man" and the two of them burst into laughter.

"I'm sorry but I needed that." Nina was still laughing,

"Do you want to hear this or what?" Topaz tried to pretend like she was mad. She fastened the diaper and slapped Turquoise playfully on the tush.

"Go on." Nina pulled the baby across the bed and tickled her. "Things are all good with you and Keisha and . . ."

"I think she's going to help me get back together with Germain."

"Really? Keisha knows Germain?"

"Yes. Their families have been friends forever. That's why she got so mad at me because she said I used Germain."

"How you ever left that fine man for Gunther is beyond me. No offense, Turkey, but your daddy was an idiot."

"I was brain-damaged. Please . . . don't even go there."

"Say, how did it go in court? Was that Carmen Electra hoochie there?"

"Martinez. Yes, she was there with Gunther's sister and the press."

"The press?"

"Nina, I don't want to talk about that now. I'm getting my baby back. I prayed for this. I said if there is a God in heaven . . . please help me get back with Germain."

"There's a God in heaven. So when are you going to see Germain?"

"I don't know. Keisha said he was in Sweden at a conference but he should be back soon and I can see my baby boy."

"Chris . . . how old is he now?"

"Almost eight."

"Wow . . . that's really great, Topaz. I've got some news too."

"What?" She stretched out on the California king next to Nina and put her daughter in between them, ready to hear some tidbit of juicy gossip that Nina had picked up somewhere.

"I got my classes."

"Is that all?"

Nina sighed and took the ring box out of her purse and gave it to Topaz. "And I got this. . . ."

Topaz opened the case and gasped. "Nina, this is an engagement ring."

"I know."

"It's beautiful. Why aren't you wearing it?" Topaz took it out of the box and tried it on. "Girl, are you crazy?"

"Give me that." She pulled the ring from Topaz's slender finger. "I haven't even tried it on yet."

"Why not?" Topaz was shocked.

"Because I haven't given him an answer."

"What are you waiting for? You know it's going to be yes. Jamil loves you. Here, put it on." Topaz slid the ring on Nina's finger. "That sucker will blind you but it fits perfectly."

Nina looked at the ring on her finger, removed it, and returned it to the box. "It's a beautiful ring, but I don't want to get married now."

"You guys aren't getting married tomorrow. It takes time to plan a wedding."

"I like being single. He's talking about kids. I'm not ready for all of that."

"You don't have to have kids right away. You'll have plenty of time for that. You guys can take time and enjoy each other."

"But I don't know if I want all of that."

"What do you want?"

"For now I just want to take my writing classes, drive my new truck, go shopping . . . I don't know. I need to take my time and find out what I want."

"But can't you do that with Jamil?"

Nina sighed as she watched her cousin tickle the baby until they both screamed with laughter.

How can I expect you to understand when I don't even understand?

She took the ring box and carefully placed it in her nightstand.

Chapter Five

Keisha walked with Kendra out to the small yellow school bus, parked in front of the house, that transported Kendra back and forth to private school. She handed her daughter her favorite *Hello, Kitty* lunch box, planted a kiss on top of her head, and watched her take a seat beside her new friend, Tyree. She threw up a hand to wave good-bye but Kendra and Tyree were too busy playing Tetris to notice.

She sighed and walked back into the house that was already organized and spotless. Keisha had wasted no time unpacking and settling her family into their home in Ladera Heights Estates. She wanted them comfortable with all their personal paraphernalia at hand.

With nothing pressing to do, she went into the family room and flipped on the television set. She almost wished she were still home-schooling Kendra just to give her something constructive to do, but she had elected to send the child to school to meet new playmates. She sat there staring at the television feeling like an idiot.

I'm bored. I need something to do.

She jumped up and gazed out the window. The house offered a panoramic view of the city and when it was clear she could see the

Pacific Ocean, which was rare in Smog City. She opened the screen door and stepped out onto the deck. It was chilly and the crisp air was soothing.

Keisha's boredom wasn't anything new. She had wrestled with it ever since Kendra began full days at school and now it pulled and nagged her constantly. She hadn't shared these feelings with anyone, especially Eric. She never wanted him to think she was unhappy, but she had to find something to do. She could always go shopping, but even that got old. She needed something meaningful and fulfilling.

She had never pursued any of her own dreams. She didn't even know what they were anymore. She had delayed going straight to college, choosing to work for her father. She had kept track of various research grants and budgets for his research in sickle cell disease. Dr. Melvyn Nichols had a thriving practice as a hematologist, but in recent years had dedicated himself to finding a cure for the illness that primarily affected children in the African-American community.

Dr. Nichols was constantly called upon for speaking engagements, fund-raisers, and dinners. Keisha had also been responsible for the annual Christmas party in the Edward Nichols wing of the Children's Hospital, named in memory of her grandfather, who had also been a hematologist. It was a never-ending project soliciting various corporations and local businesses to donate toys and games for the children, and celebrities to attend and sign autographs. That was all before she took a trip to New York City with Topaz and met Eric. The rest, as they say, is history.

Jade had touched a sensitive spot in her when she voiced her objection to Keisha *only* being a wife and a mother. To be a good wife and a good mother was a full-time job. Was she less of a person because she had committed herself solely to her family? Was it her fault that her husband made more than enough money to take care of his family? Why did she feel so guilty for being so blessed? For some reason she was angry and she didn't know why.

She didn't realize she was shivering until she felt her teeth chattering. She was standing in front of the fireplace warming herself when Eric walked in.

"Hi, sweetie, how was practice?" She sprang into his arms and greeted him with a kiss.

"Pretty good. I hope I get a chance to play tonight." He pulled her closer and nuzzled her cheek. "You're shaking," he observed immediately. "What's wrong?"

"I was standing outside looking at the view before you came in and I got a little chilled. I'll be okay as soon as I get warm."

"You have to be careful here, Key, not to catch cold. It's wintertime. Why were you outside without a coat?"

"I just stepped outside and started thinking about things I need to take care of."

"What things?" He led her to the sofa and tucked a colorful quilt around her.

"Just some things I need to take care of around the house. Would you make me a cup of apple tea, sweetie?" She hoped the tea would end his fishing expedition. She didn't want him asking questions that she was trying to answer herself.

"Sure, baby." He sprang to his feet and put on the teakettle.

"Your daughter has a boyfriend. She was so busy with him once she got on the bus, she didn't even notice me."

"I'll kill 'em." Eric handed her the tea and sat down beside her while Keisha giggled and sipped the hot tea.

"You're funny."

"I'm serious." Eric wasn't smiling and Keisha laughed even more.

"I'm glad she has a new friend. She can't wait to see Chris and Germain, too. I wonder if he's back yet."

"Who?"

"Germain Gradney. You know he lives here, too, in Pacific Palisades."

"That's right. I forgot about the good doctor. I bet he's making bank out here in the cosmetic surgery business."

"I'm sure he is. He's been in Sweden. Topaz wants me to help her get back with him."

"Ms. Topaz . . . now there's a piece of work."

"Eric, stop. She's my friend."

"If you say so . . . but I wouldn't get involved in that. I gotta get some rest before the game. Don't let me oversleep." He kissed her and he was gone.

Keisha had never felt so alone in the crowd at the Staples Center. She looked at Shaq and Kobe running up and down the court and then at Eric waiting patiently on the bench for an opportunity to play, and whispered a prayer.

She knew her husband wanted to be out there in the game, not warming the bench. Kendra, dressed like a little Laker cheerleader, was adorable. It was Friday night, a family night whenever there was a home game. She felt strange sitting by herself in the stands. In New York, they would pig out on popcorn, hot dogs, and soda. Her heart ached for her friends and she wished there was someone to talk to.

The coach called a time-out and the Laker girls ran out onto the floor to perform a quick routine. Keisha looked around at the people sitting near her and recognized a few of the other players' wives. They were all so glamorous with impeccable makeup and sophisticated designer clothing.

Keisha never wore makeup except for lipstick and mascara and she wondered if her jeans and sweater counted as proper attire for the wife of a Laker. Just about everyone on the team was a household name and Eric would be, too, once he started getting minutes.

These LA women look like stars.

She watched two gorgeous women saunter by in tight dresses and suddenly remembered something Celeste had said.

"Ain't no hoochie like an LA hoochie."

There were always women hanging around trying to get close to the players and it didn't matter if a player was married. The women didn't care. These women were bold and believed any wife was replaceable.

Eric had never been unfaithful to her or even given her cause to wonder. But Celeste had been adamant when she also said, *"They all tip and slip eventually."*

The buzzer sounded and the guys were back on the floor and Eric was with them. God had answered her prayer.

"Look at Daddy, baby." Keisha pointed him out to Kendra and everyone cheered when Eric tossed in a much-needed three-pointer.

"You go, baby." She yelled until her throat hurt but she didn't care. That was her man and she was proud of him. He was hot tonight. Keisha knew he felt her spirit urging him on to victory. He had told her he could feel her and he always played better when she was in attendance.

His black Range Rover pulled into the driveway just minutes behind Keisha. She had stopped to pick up her husband's favorite Fatburger with an egg, chili, and cheese.

"You won, Daddy. You won. The game was boring until you tossed in all those three-pointers." Kendra sat in his lap and took a bite of his hamburger.

"Spoken like a true fan." Keisha laughed and poured champagne into flutes for them and a little glass of ginger ale for Kendra. "Okay, little girl, drink up and then it's upstairs to bed."

"I have to make a toast first." Kendra was serious as she picked up her glass while Keisha and Eric exchanged glances and tried not to laugh.

"To my Daddy, the bestest player on the Lakers."

"I'll drink to that." Keisha touched glasses with her family.

Once upstairs, Eric heard Kendra's prayers while Keisha warmed vanilla body oil for his massage. She smiled as she rubbed the oil into his smooth skin.

"My baby's got some anointed fingers."

She felt his body relax at the touch of her hands and smiled. She knew it would be a matter of minutes before he was asleep, but he always woke her up before morning so they could play.

Keisha curled up next to him and waited for his strong arm to clasp her to his side. It never ceased to amaze her how he reached for her, even when he was sound asleep. She lay next to him feeling the warmth of his body and listened to his breathing.

I've got to get Topaz to take me shopping for makeup and new clothes. She stroked Eric's chin and drifted off to sleep.

Chapter Six

Jade sat in her studio overlooking the Pacific Ocean in Santa Barbara. It was very early and the tide was still out. She had crept in at the brink of dawn while Sean and the rest of the world were asleep. There was something sacred about the birth of a new day . . . it was a gift from God, to be celebrated, and Jade felt honored to behold its splendor.

She was almost afraid to breathe as she watched the heavens transform like a kaleidoscope from a velvety midnight blue into azure flecked with rose and purple. She had intended to read a few scriptures and catch up on her journal, but this was a moment worth capturing.

Not wanting to disturb the serenity of her waterfront sanctuary, Jade tiptoed across the room and placed a fresh canvas on her easel. She opened a tin of watercolors and deliberated carefully before selecting several tubes and squeezing globs of paint on a palette. She blended and mixed colors until she had duplicated those in the sunrise. People never ceased to marvel over the intensity of her work, but she thought it all too easy when all she did was paint what she saw . . . God was the master when it came to artistry.

The sun was blazing when she stepped back to admire the painting. She smiled, pleased with the finished result. She was stretching in front of the window when she saw Sean jogging across the beach on the damp sand, and she stopped to watch him run. He moved gracefully with an easy, even gait. The white sweats on his dark, beautiful body, rippling with muscles, made a striking combination. She pressed her face against the glass until he was no longer in view.

Jade knew how Sean loved the tranquility of their Santa Barbara home, and had made the sacrifice of living in Los Angeles for her. He could easily stay away from the city with its maze of congested freeways, smog, and crime forever. Jade, however, though she loved the escape when she wanted to create, thrived on the energy of the city.

She had purchased several novels for her husband before they left the city. Sean could lose himself in a book for hours, so she was surprised when she saw him walking across the room toward her instead of reading on the deck. Occasionally, she ran with him, but they enjoyed separate interests and quiet time apart.

"Hi, honey. Did you enjoy your run on the beach?" She smiled at him before placing a fresh canvas on the easel.

"I sure did. I've missed my beach and it was exactly what I needed." He picked up a stool and sat down behind her.

"That's good." She took a charcoal and deftly sketched in sweeping motions across the canvas. He watched, fascinated.

"I love watching you paint. You make it look so easy."

"I enjoyed watching you run down the beach. You look so fine I started to come outside and jump your bones." Sean grinned while she continued to sketch.

"You should have." He scooted up behind her and caressed her protruding belly. "How are you, little boy? Daddy can't wait to hold you." He sat there holding Jade when the baby kicked.

"Jade, baby, he kicked. He heard me talking to him and he kicked. He knows his daddy's voice." He was too proud. In his excitement, he bumped his wife's arm.

"Sean, look what you did. This is an important new piece." She took her ball of art gum and attempted to erase the unwanted stroke.

"I'm sorry, honey. Can't you fix it?" He was genuinely concerned as he watched her rub out the line.

"I think so." She frowned and brushed away some loose particles.

"Good." He sat back down behind her.

"You can't sit here. You're in my way. Don't you have a book to read or something?"

"I have a book but you've been in here working all morning. I thought we came up here to relax."

"I am relaxing." She dug in a tray for another piece of charcoal.

"You're painting as usual. I want to do something together. Let's go window-shopping in the village or go see a movie." He was trying hard to remain calm.

"Maybe later, sweetie. I want to finish this."

"You always have to finish something and everything is always more important than me." He was practically pouting.

"Sean . . ." She was surprised by his outburst. "You know that's not true. I've just been very busy lately. Things will get back to normal soon. Now go, so I can finish." She glanced up at him to see his expression. He was standing in front of the sunrise painting that she'd completed earlier.

"I thought you were going to start using Ross on your work. You just finished this and you signed it Kimura."

"All right, Sean, get out of here. You're trying to start a fight and I am not in the mood for your silliness today."

"Silliness? What's so silly about a wife using her husband's last name?"

"I'm known as Jade Kimura. My gallery that you gave me as a birthday present is the Jade Kimura gallery. So why would I change my name to Jade Ross now?" She faced him, waiting for a response.

"You could go by Jade Kimura Ross."

"That takes up too much space. Everyone knows I'm your wife. I can't even go to the Smithsonian without some stupid fan of yours asking me to sign a stupid basketball. So why are you tripping?" Now she was angry.

"Maybe I'd trip a little less if you paid as much attention to me as you do to your work. Why can't you be a wife like Keisha?"

"Keisha?" She could barely say her name. "That boring cow? How dare you compare me to her? She needs to get a life."

"So do you, sweetheart. So do you."

He left before she could say another word. She heard him outside moments later shooting hoops. She tossed the canvas across the room and burst into tears. She hated to fight with her husband.

I tried so hard not to let him get to me this time and somehow he always does. He knew I was an artist with a career before he married me. I'm not giving up my work.

She retrieved her canvas and felt herself relax as soon as she began working. She could still hear Sean's basketball bouncing on the pavement when she cleaned her brushes.

Someone's got to be the bigger person. She went into the kitchen and juiced carrots and apples, got a bottle of Evian, and carried everything outside and sat on a bench by the edge of the court. He was soaking wet and had been playing for several hours. She picked up his towel and carried it to him with the water. She handed him the towel and he drank the water in a series of gulps.

"Maybe you should come in now. It's getting chilly and I don't want you to catch cold."

"Why, because I might give it to you and then you'd have to cancel one of your precious appointments?"

Jade could hear the pain in his voice and he looked like a rejected child. He was hurting and she hated to think she had caused him pain. She pulled him into her arms and kissed him.

"No, because I love you. Now come inside."

He allowed her to lead him inside and into the bathroom. She had lit dozens of scented candles around a tub spilling over with bubbles, and Luther was playing softly in the background. She undressed him and then herself. They sat facing each other immersed in swirling fragrant water.

"This is nice." He finally spoke.

"It is. Especially with you here." She thought she saw a hint of a smile. "I'm sorry, baby. I know you wanted us to spend time together this weekend and I took advantage of us being here and used the time to paint."

"I'm sorry, too, baby. I'm a spoiled brat."

"You are, but you're my spoiled brat. I'm a little spoiled, too."

"A little?" Sean smiled and she felt her insides melt like butter.

"Okay." She laughed. "A lot."

They sat in front of the fireplace later, wearing bathrobes and eating his favorite Mexican food. Jade had ordered a feast of guacamole, chips and salsa, shrimp tacos and burritos, and refried pintos oozing with melted Monterey Jack cheese and green onions.

"I feel like such a pig." She pushed away the tin of pintos. She liked to eat them with chips and salsa.

"You are. Just make sure you keep my boy satisfied." He rubbed her stomach and the baby kicked. "See, I told you he knows me."

"He sure does." Jade smiled while he massaged her belly. She climbed into his lap and felt herself nodding. The one good thing about fighting was they had so much fun making up.

"Baby, I've been thinking about something and I wanted to know how you feel about it." He kissed her gently on the neck.

"What were you thinking, sweetie?" She was practically asleep.

"You know it's only been a year since I retired, but I've been thinking about coming out of retirement and playing basketball again."

"Really?" Her eyes flew open; she was wide-awake now.

"Yeah, with the Lakers. So we'd be right here in LA."

"Sean, that's a fabulous idea and a perfect solution. You need something to keep you busy while I'm working."

Chapter Seven

Topaz balanced Turquoise on her hip while she pulled a stroller out of the back of her Range Rover. "Mama's gonna buy her baby a new pair of shoes." She pushed her daughter toward the elevators at the Beverly Center, looking every bit the diva in jeans, boots, and a sweater. Her makeup was flawless and her hair was pulled back in a single braid under a cowboy hat.

Keisha couldn't believe what she was seeing. She stood by the car with Kendra, wondering if this was really her friend, Topaz, and how she managed to look so glamorous and be a mother.

"Keisha, why are you standing there?" Topaz yelled over her shoulder. "I'm ready to shop."

Heads turned and people stared, but Topaz was oblivious as she walked through the mall with purpose. "You wanted to get some makeup?" She pushed the stroller into the MAC store.

"Yes . . ." Keisha wasn't sounding very sure.

"Why? You always looked so pretty without it." Topaz examined the new eye shadows and rubbed a golden powder on her hand.

"I thought I'd try something new," Keisha practically whispered.

"Do you know what colors you want?"

"No, that's why I asked you to come. You know I don't know

anything about makeup. That gold eye shadow was very pretty on you."

"It would look even prettier on you." Topaz took a brush and dusted the shadow across Keisha's eyelids. "That looks so pretty." She handed her a hand mirror and watched a smile light up her friend's face when she saw her reflection.

"I like." Keisha grinned. "What about some of this?" She pointed to face powder and blush.

"You want all that, too?"

"Girl, I want the works."

Topaz picked up Turquoise and bounced her up and down on her hip while she supervised Keisha's selections. She sat there watching both of their daughters while a makeup artist gave Keisha a new look.

"You're looking mighty gorgeous, Key." Topaz blended the blush on her high cheekbones. "Wait until Eric sees you."

"I hope he likes it." She handed the clerk a Visa and looked to Topaz for affirmation.

"How could he not like it? You look very glamorous and sophisticated."

"Good." Keisha smiled, relieved. "Now let's go clothes shopping.

"Okay, what's up, girl? Why the new look? Did Eric tell you to start wearing makeup?" Topaz helped Kendra to stand up on the baby's stroller so she could ride, too. Turquoise laughed and tried to push her off.

"Eric's wonderful. He didn't tell me to wear makeup. It's just that everyone in LA is so glamorous. The players' wives and girlfriends look like fashion models." They paused to look at the Coach bags.

"So . . . you do, too. I was always jealous of that hourglass shape and the way you always looked so pretty with no makeup."

"You jealous of me? You were the beautiful one with all that long hair and those light eyes. We couldn't go anywhere without some brother trying to hit on you."

40

Topaz looked at her friend. "Don't you think you're pretty, Key?"

"I hadn't given it a lot of thought until recently. People are really into looking beautiful here and I want to feel beautiful, too. I knew things would change when we moved here."

"Maybe it's not things that are changing, but you, Key."

Keisha looked at Topaz to be sure it was she that had spoken. The trademark golden eyes stared back. She couldn't believe how much Topaz had changed . . . for the better. "You sound like Karla."

"Who's Karla?"

"My best friend in Jersey. She's married to one of Sean's brothers."

"He has brothers? Are they as fine as him?"

"Yes, and they're identical twins."

"I'm hungry, Mommy. Can we eat lunch now?" Kendra looked at Keisha with pleading eyes.

"She looks just like you, Key. And she's so good." Topaz led them into the California Pizza Kitchen.

"Turquoise looks just like you, too. She even has those golden eyes. I can't believe how well she speaks for being so young." Keisha stroked the little girl's bronze ponytail.

Topaz pulled a slice of pizza out of the pie and licked the hot cheese from her fingers. "My cousin Nina reads all the time and she reads to her every night. Nina polishes her fingernails. They watch videos and play games. She's always with one of us."

"Kendra's always with me, too, but she's a daddy's girl. She's a good little traveling companion." She placed another slice of pizza on her daughter's plate. "So how are things with your court case?"

Topaz stopped chewing. "Didn't I tell you Carmen Electra posed for Playboy?"

"Carmen Electra?"

"Carmen Martinez. Nina calls her Carmen Electra and now she's got me doing it. Playboy paid her some ridiculous amount of money and she took it all off."

"What?" Keisha squealed and covered her mouth with a napkin. "Tell me you're kidding."

"Nope. And every time they write about her, they mention my name. So now I'm in Playboy. I blame Gunther's lowlife family for everything."

"This world is crazy. You do something wrong and they make you a star."

"Tell me about it. Some people will do anything for money and fame."

Back in the mall, Topaz led Keisha into DKNY. "You know this had to be one of my favorite stores. Remember that night we were at the mall and I was drooling over Donna Karan and I met Mick?"

"That seems like ages ago. I thought Mick was a stalker and he wanted you to pose for *Mademoiselle*. That was the last time we went shopping."

"This would be so cute on you." Topaz held up a black linen skirt and top trimmed in leather. "Go try it on."

Topaz sat outside the dressing room and played with the girls while Keisha tried on the outfit. "Remember when I was the one trying on the clothes and you were sitting out here?"

"Yes." Keisha laughed. She stepped out of the dressing room and posed. "What do you think?" She turned around so Topaz could see how the skirt fit across her butt.

"You look hot. But then you already knew that or you would have never let me see it on you, heifer." Keisha laughed and Topaz joined in.

"You look pretty, Mommy." Kendra sat on Topaz's lap and watched her mother primp in the mirror.

"Thank you, sweetheart." She kissed Kendra on the cheek. "I'm going to take these braids out of my hair, too. It's time for a change."

"I'll take you to my hairdresser. She's great with cuts and color. Try these on, too." Topaz tossed her a pair of butter-soft, black leather pants and a jacket.

"I'm glad we did this. I had so much fun today."

"Yeah, me too."

"But you didn't even buy anything." Keisha walked out in the black leather.

"Aw, suki, suki. Look out, LA, Keisha Johnson is here." Topaz stood next to her in the mirror and smiled. "Look at us ... you married to a big NBA star and me a famous singer. Did you ever think we'd be this rich?"

"Yes." Topaz answered for them while Keisha shook her head to say no.

"I've missed you so much." Topaz hugged her friend. "My only real friend is Nina. She's like a sister."

"I've missed you, too." Keisha was surprised to see tears in Topaz's eyes. She quickly wiped a tear from her eye, and laughed when she saw Kendra hugging the baby.

"You are so lucky, Key. You got it all. A wonderful man who loves you, a beautiful daughter, and we can't forget that you're a millionaire."

"You're right. God has blessed me and I thank Him every day. You had it all, too. I was only trying to be like you."

"I did have it all, didn't I? But you're smart enough to know when you've got it all. Don't be stupid like me." The joy faded from Topaz's face and she plopped down in the chair.

"Stop being so hard on yourself. You'll have it all again."

Topaz glanced up at Keisha, waiting to see what she would say next.

"I believe Germain still loves you. You'll get him back, and I'm going to help you."

"You will?"

"Of course I will. Isn't that what friends are for?"

Chapter Eight

Nina read the copy from the teleprompter as if she had been doing it all her life. It was chilly in the studio and she was glad she had worn the red suede dress that she had been saving for something special. Jamil had said to look sexy, but professional.

She hadn't been the least bit interested when Jamil had phoned last night to inform her that he had gotten her an interview for a job with MTV. She knew it was just another ploy to get her away from writing and back in the music industry, but she had consented to go to the audition to keep peace, especially since she hadn't given him an answer to his marriage proposal yet.

The network's producers wanted a Hollywood correspondent to cover award shows, parties, and premieres for a news-oriented talk show. She had faxed them several writing samples this morning and now she stood there talking to the camera.

"That was great." The lights faded and a young man with a clipboard wearing a headset appeared from nowhere.

"Thanks." Nina smiled and wondered if she was chilly or nervous.

"Are you an actress, Nina?" He studied her carefully and made some notes.

"No." She hoped her voice hadn't revealed her annoyance with the question.

Can't a girl be pretty and not be a singer, dancer, model, or an actress in this city?

"I was the personal assistant to Topaz."

"Really? What was it like working for her?" It was hard to see his eyes with the glare on his glasses.

"Extremely busy, but fun." She stared at the spot on his glasses where she thought his eyes were.

"I can see I'm not going to get any dirt from you." He laughed. "So why did you leave?" He was writing on the clipboard again.

Because my cousin wouldn't let me have a life. . . .

"I wanted to take some writing classes. I didn't think I would be able to do them both well." She flashed a Pepsodent smile.

A handsome blond joined him and smiled at Nina.

"Ms. Beaubien, this is Wes Chandler, our executive producer." They whispered momentarily and the one wearing the eyeglasses left.

"I'm sorry for the interruption, Nina, I just have one final question." He smiled, displaying perfectly even teeth.

He is fine. Nina returned the smile.

"Why do you want to work for MTV?"

Because my boyfriend told me to come and now I want the job. . . . Why do people ask such dumb questions on interviews?

"I want to write." Nina heard herself and realized she had spoken. "I want new experiences. I love people and I love music."

"Thanks for coming, Nina. Good luck with your writing."

She felt a wave of disappointment flood her body. Now that she had done an interview and understood what the job was about, she really wanted it. As she headed for her car, her cell phone rang before she could put the key in the ignition.

"How did you do on the interview, baby?" She was surprised to hear from Jamil. He had told her that he would be in meetings all day.

"I did okay, I guess. Why didn't you tell me they wanted writing samples? I had to stay up late and make something up."

"I know you gave them what they needed. You got skills, baby."

"I just wish I had been more prepared. I had to act like I was hosting the news."

"Baby, why are you tripping? I know you looked good."

She looked at the red suede dress. "I hope I wore the right thing. I didn't think I wanted to work, but I would have liked this job."

"I know you would. That's why when my girl at *MTV* told me about it, I knew it was just the thing for my baby."

"Thanks, Jamil. I'm glad you thought about me even if I don't get the job." She started the truck.

"I think about you all the time." His tone was sincere. "You coming over tonight?"

"Probably . . . but you come by the house. I feel like cooking."

Nina pushed the shopping cart to the back of the market and inspected the meat and seafood behind the glass counter.

What can I make to go with potato salad?

She had the butcher cut up two chickens for frying and purchased several pounds of red snapper. Nina enjoyed cooking.

I wonder how much I would like it if I had to cook daily. . . .

Ever since Jamil had proposed, she tried to imagine what it would be like to be married with a family, what it would be like to not work. She could never stay home and just cook.

I'd definitely have a cook and a maid.

She picked up several more items and paid for her groceries.

I love being single.

Nina enjoyed her independence . . . making her own money and her own decisions. She did what she wanted when she wanted.

If Jamil think he's going to put a sister on lockdown . . .

She tied an apron on and washed and seasoned the chicken and fish and prepared the potato salad. She had just placed a casserole of macaroni and cheese in the oven and was dropping pieces of chicken into the hot cooking oil when Topaz and Turquoise came in.

"Nina, you're cooking. . . ." Topaz looked at her cousin and grinned.

"I felt like throwing together a little something." She turned over the chicken and it sizzled as juices from the meat diffused through the hot oil.

"You are going to be such a good wife for Jamil." Topaz left the kitchen to take Turquoise upstairs to her nanny before Nina could answer.

A good wife.

She removed the chicken, placed it on a platter to cool, and dropped in the red snapper.

"It smells so good in here. Can I have a piece of chicken?" Topaz stood next to her eyeing a wing and Nina put it on a plate for her. She sat at the table, pulled the wing apart, and bit into it.

"This is so good, Nina. You haven't cooked for a long time."

"I've been busy. I was just thinking about what it would be like to be married and have to cook every day."

"That's an interesting concept. How about some champagne for you to cook with?" Topaz opened the refrigerator and uncorked a fresh bottle. "I went shopping with Keisha today."

Thank God for Keisha.

Ever since their reunion, Topaz had loosened her grip on her.

"We picked out clothes and makeup. She was feeling a little insecure about the women in LA. She said everyone is so gorgeous. But Key is beautiful, inside and out."

"Women are always after those ballplayers. She has a lot to deal with. What kind of guy is Eric?" She took the macaroni and cheese out of the oven and Topaz squealed.

"We're going into the gym as soon as we finish eating." Topaz served herself a helping of everything. "Ever since I had Turquoise I have to exercise more."

"I exercised this morning but Jamil is always talking about my butt. It has gotten bigger."

That's another thing. . . . You have kids and you have to watch your weight.

"But it's tight. You could flip a quarter on that thing."

"Don't even go there, or I'll fry chicken and make potato salad every day." Nina laughed. "You know you have no control when it comes to food."

"You are so wrong. . . . You asked me about Eric. He seemed like a very sweet guy, but I don't really know him. Keisha really loves him."

"Do you think she lost her identity?" Nina put another piece of fish on her plate and doused it with hot sauce.

"What do you mean?" Topaz stopped chewing and focused her amber eyes on her cousin.

"If a woman doesn't have interests other than her man, she can get so absorbed into him that she loses perspective of who she is."

"Wow . . . I wonder if that's what happened to Key. She always had so much confidence when we were growing up. She didn't go to college; she was working for her father. She didn't have to work because they had money, but she was always real smart. I think she always wanted to be married."

"And she married money . . . nothing wrong with that. A lot of those ballers just want their wives to take care of them and have babies. Jamil would love for me to do that."

"I'd do that for Germain."

"You'd give up your career and never set foot on a stage or in a studio again? You'd just stay home and have his babies?" Nina folded her arms across her chest and looked at her cousin.

"In a heartbeat."

"You're serious, aren't you?"

"As a heart attack. Success is great but you need someone to share it with."

Is this my cousin?

Nina watched Topaz as she got up to answer the phone.

"It's MTV," Topaz whispered loudly, covering the phone with her hand. "Why are they calling you about me? If it's that Carmen Martinez crap . . ."

"Everything is not always about you." She took the phone and after several minutes of conversation, a huge smile lit up her face.

"I have a new job. I'm MTV's Hollywood correspondent."

Chapter Nine

Keisha carefully outlined her full lips with the new pencil the way Topaz had shown her, then covered them with red lipstick. She was quite pleased with her reflection even though she didn't like the feel of the foundation on her face.

"Keisha, hurry up, baby. I'm hungry."

"I'll be right there, sweetie." She wanted to surprise Eric so she had made him wait downstairs while she finished dressing. He had the night off and they were going to a jazz club for dinner at Manhattan Beach.

She pulled the hot rollers from her hair and smiled when she saw the highlights. Topaz's hairstylist had removed the braids and layered her shoulder-length hair. Keisha loved the fullness and the way every strand fell back into place when she shook her head. She looked over her collection of perfumes, searching for the perfect scent. Some she had chosen just because the bottles were so pretty, but this was a night for Allure. She stepped into her heels and headed for the stairs.

Eric was watching Emeril prepare a steak dish and he was practically salivating.

"No wonder you're so hungry." She couldn't help laughing as

she draped a cheetah-print scarf around her shoulders and he cut off the television.

"I'm starvin' like Marvin. You ready to go?" He turned around and she was standing there looking too sensational. "Dang, baby, you are fine."

Keisha couldn't contain her smile when his voice hit a note two octaves higher than usual.

"You like?" She smiled and slowly turned around so he could see the way the black skirt gently hugged her voluptuous curves.

"Oh yeah . . ." He grinned and kissed her softly behind the ear.

"Let's go, Eric. If you keep that up we won't go out to dinner, and you said you were hungry."

"I am hungry . . . for a lot of things." He licked his lips and grinned. "Are you sure you want to go out to dinner?"

"Boy, you are so nasty." She laughed, loving every minute of it.

They took the Porsche, and Eric couldn't keep his eyes or his hands off of her the entire night. They were adventurous and ordered paella and sangria, after they had stuffed themselves with shrimp ceviche and fresh, hot tortilla chips. They loved to try new foods and California presented them with a wealth of fine cuisines to experience. Eric, unlike the typical meat-and-potatoes-only man, would try anything once.

He poured the last of the sangria into their glasses and moved Keisha's chair so they were side by side, and so she could get a better view of the quartet. The sangria had mellowed her and she rested her head on his shoulder. She felt as if she were in heaven listening to soft, soothing jazz, coupled with a view of the moon shining on the ocean.

"So what's up with this new look?" He fingered a lock of her hair.

"I just wanted to try something new." She stroked the back of his hand. "I thought you liked it."

"I do. I love it. But you know I love you anyway and in everything."

"You do, baby?" She kissed him softly on the lips.

"Of course I do. I was just wondering if this new look had anything to do with Topaz."

"Topaz? You know me better than that." She sat up straight in her chair, promising herself she wouldn't get upset.

"I know. I just don't want you going Hollywood on me and turning into some sort of diva."

"You think I would do something like that?" She heard her voice squeak and wondered how they had gone from being so romantic to this.

"No, baby." He looked at her with those sweet honey eyes and she felt herself melting.

"So where is all this coming from?" She rested her head back on his shoulder and took his hand in hers.

"Sean was talking about Jade. She's going through a lot of changes. I just don't want you changing on me. I like my girl, Key, just the way she is." He kissed her with so much passion she blushed.

"My boy's feeling a little neglected. Do you think you could talk to Jade, give her a few tips on the down-low?"

"I'd be glad to talk to her, but Jade and I aren't close at all. I wouldn't feel comfortable talking to her about something so personal. I was really looking forward to spending time with her and I can barely stand being around her."

"You're kidding!"

"No, sweetie, she has changed. She's really full of herself and her work. I thought it was me, and then I thought it might be the pregnancy. Now you're saying Sean is unhappy."

"I didn't say all that."

"Well, something's up. What exactly did he say?"

"Nothing much, but something's bothering him. I tried to get him to talk about it and we ended up talking about golf. I can't believe Jade doesn't like you." Eric really looked bothered.

"Come on, sweetie, there's nothing we can do now. I'll think about it. Let's enjoy ourselves. Wasn't it nice of Topaz to keep Kendra so we could spend some time alone?"

"Yeah, it was nice of her, but I can't believe Topaz is watching her." Eric ordered lattes and bananas royale.

"I haven't heard from our daughter since she called to say Nina was helping her with her homework, and that Topaz has a movie theater in her house, so they were going to watch *Dr. Dolittle* when she finished.

"A movie theater?" Eric laughed. "Now she'll come home wanting me to put one in our house. Does Topaz have a nanny?"

"Yes, but she takes care of Turquoise herself. She even took her to the mall when we went shopping."

"Really? Now I'm impressed."

"You are so bad." Keisha laughed. "She's really changed, Eric. Sometimes I can't believe she's the same girl I grew up with in Atlanta."

"Miss Thing? The Queen of Drama? Changed? I'd have to see it to believe it. Your girl always has an agenda. I'm not as sweet and trusting as you." He kissed her on the lips.

"I trust Topaz. She just needed to grow up. That's why I'm going to help her get back together with Germain."

"Are you sure you want to get involved in that?"

"Yes. I want to invite them to dinner. You don't mind, do you?" She felt herself grow a little warm. She had never thought Eric would have any objection to her wanting to play Cupid.

"No, I don't mind, baby. If it hadn't been for Topaz, I wouldn't have met you. Why don't you invite Jade and Sean, too?"

"Jade and Sean? That's an idea. A dinner party may be just the thing to break the ice. You're a genius, sweetie." She kissed him on the lips. "This may be the very reason why the Lord sent us out here."

"To meddle in other people's business? Okay, Miss Cupid . . . whatever you want to do, I'm behind you . . . I just have one request." He smiled at her with twinkling eyes.

"What?" She smiled back.

"Can we go home now so I can peel you out of that skirt?"

* * *

The next morning during her prayer time with Karla, she shared some of the previous night's events and her plans for the dinner party.

"I'm so excited, Karla. I know this is why God sent us out here . . . so we can help our friends."

Chapter Ten

Jade felt the baby give her a swift kick as she took her foot and closed the door to the Marina penthouse. She juggled a bag of groceries in each hand and a portfolio case under her arm.

I sure will be glad when he's out of me and things get back to normal.

"Why didn't you get the doorman to help you or phone me before you got out of the car?"

Sean leaped to his feet to relieve her of the bags and in the process he let the art case drop on the floor. She hadn't seen him sitting in the den, but she should have known he was somewhere in the house because the television was on.

Why is he always sitting around here?

"You know you shouldn't have tried to carry all these things by yourself in your condition. You act like you're not pregnant. There's no reason for you to carry these things when there are people around to help you."

She glanced at him as she picked up her portfolio and quickly unzipped it to make sure nothing had been damaged.

She walked into the kitchen behind him, hoping he hadn't peeked in the bags that contained ingredients for the Jamaican dinner she had planned as a surprise for him.

"Why are you here? I thought you had an appointment."

"It was canceled and it was a good thing. You could have hurt yourself trying to carry all those things. What's this for?" He held up a plantain and grinned. "Are you cooking tonight?"

"Don't you have anything to do?" She made a face and snatched up the fruit, which she would fry and serve with rice and peas, curried vegetables, and his favorite jerk chicken.

"I've been craving fried plantain. And rum raisin ice cream and coconut cake." She managed to sneak the rest of the items into the refrigerator except for the ice cream, which he dug into with a spoon. Jade allowed him to eat a spoonful of his favorite flavor of Häagen-Dazs before she took the container from him and placed it in the freezer.

"Sean, get out of the kitchen," she yelled, pretending to be mad. "You are such a pest." He laughed and sat down in the breakfast nook where he could keep an eye on Jade, when the telephone rang.

"Hey, Keisha, what's up, girl?" Jade made a face the moment she heard him say her name. She could tell from his conversation that Keisha was returning his call. She put the chicken in the oven and sat down at the table opposite him with a fresh coconut and a hammer.

"I'm going to be out of town on business for a couple of days and I would really appreciate it if you could stay over here with Jade while I'm away. I don't want her to be here alone and I'll feel so much better knowing she's with you."

"No way is she staying here," Jade whispered loudly as she poured the milk from the coconut into a bowl and began shredding some of the meat. He seemingly ignored her as she stood in his face gesturing and giving him dirty looks.

"She's right here. I'll put her on the phone so you guys can work out all the details." His dazzling smile had no effect on the look of death she cast him when he gave her the phone. She restrained herself from taking the coconut and hitting him on the head.

"Hi, Keisha." He wrapped his arms around her and kissed all of her favorite spots and she felt herself melting.

"I only did it for your own good," he whispered in her ear with a kiss. She melted like putty from his touch.

"Eric's on a road trip so I'd love to spend some time with you. It would just be more convenient for me if you could stay over here so I don't have to move Kendra around. She gets picked up for school and she'll be more comfortable here in her own bed."

"I can come over there." Jade had no intention of going to Keisha's or calling her while Sean was out of town. She just wanted to get her off the phone so she could finish her husband's dinner.

"Thanks, baby. I won't worry if I know you're with Keisha." He kissed her on the neck as she hung up the phone.

What's wrong with me? she asked herself as they sat down to dinner. *Why am I always so upset with him?*

She had discussed her erratic mood swings with her obstetrician, who had said she was only experiencing the normal emotional and physical changes that occurred in expectant mothers.

Everyone said they should wait several years before having a baby, and take time to get to know each other, but Jade had gone against her better judgment when she didn't use any birth control on the honeymoon. She never dreamt she'd wind up pregnant.

They had discussed starting a family during premarital counseling and they both felt they were ready, despite the warning to wait. Jade wasn't even sure if they'd had intercourse properly since it was the first time and they were both virgins. Now it was more than obvious that their technique had worked very well. Jade didn't mind being pregnant. She knew Sean wanted to have a baby and she wanted to please him, but this was all before her career began to place incessant demands on her. She had to find some way to manage her husband, home, career, and baby. She was a highly intelligent, new-millennium woman. She would find a way to do it, and do it well.

Sean was packing when she went into the bedroom. She went into the laundry room, collected his clean underwear and socks that Dora had washed and pressed, and put them in his suitcase while he hung several of his favorite shirts and suits in the garment bag.

"I'll get your ties." She was sifting through the closet for matching ties when the thought of his leaving hit her like a ton of bricks and she began to cry. She was the one who usually did the traveling and this was the first time he was taking a trip without her since they had been married. Her face was covered with tears when she came out of the closet with the ties.

"Jade, baby, what's wrong? Do you feel okay?" He sat on the bed and pulled her onto his lap, where she cried like a baby.

"Jade, baby, you're scaring me. Do you want to go to the doctor?"

"No," she whimpered. "I just suddenly realized how much I'm going to miss you."

"I'll only be gone two days." His voice was kind and gentle.

"I know. I'm just being silly."

He smiled, got up and put some more logs on the fire.

"Now you know how I feel when you're always running off and leaving me."

"I never see you crying." She had finally managed to smile.

"That's 'cause I'm a man." He pounded softly on his chest. "We don't cry, we just front and tell a good lie."

Jade's laughter bubbled over like a spring. She went into the kitchen and returned with the coconut cake and rum raisin ice cream. They took turns feeding each other in the firelight.

"If my doctor hadn't told me not to fly, I'd buy a ticket and go with you." She stroked his smooth skin and black curly hair.

"I like this, you missing me." They sat in front of the fireplace, taking turns singing their favorite love songs, until the fire went out.

"I love you so much." She fought back the tears as she walked him down to the limousine because she didn't want him to feel bad because he was leaving. He wiped a tear from the corner of her eye and kissed her.

"I love you, baby. And you too, little man." He planted a kiss on her belly and patted her on the behind before he got inside the car.

"I'll go stay with Keisha, baby. I promise." Jade watched the shiny black car until it was no longer in sight.

Chapter Eleven

Topaz looked at the latest copy of the *National Enquirer* with a photograph of her with Germain and Chris on the front cover, and she screamed. A banner headline splashed across the page read TOPAZ LIVED SECRET DOUBLE LIFE.

"Oh, my God. . . . Where the hell did they get this from?"

She felt sick as she quickly read the article filled with half-truths and innuendoes. *Topaz Black Lawrence, widow of the late Gunther Lawrence, was secretly married to her Atlanta sweetheart, Dr. Germain Gradney, the father of her eight-year-old son, Christopher Black Gradney, the entire time she was married to director-producer Lawrence, best known for* The Hood *and several other box-office smashes.*

"What a pack of horrendous lies. . . . I can't read anymore." She tossed the rag sheet aside and poured herself a glass of water.

Where did they get that photo? And how did they find out about my marriage and Chris after all this time? Germain's going to hate me even more now.

She felt the hot tears sliding down her cheeks and she was angry. Her privacy had been invaded in the worst way and there was nothing she could do about it.

"How long will I have to pay for that mistake of a marriage to Gunther? How long?"

She was crying when the phone rang. She let it ring, waiting for her private answering service to pick up, and after seven rings, she finally snatched the phone up herself.

"What's wrong, sweetie?" It was Keisha, sounding very concerned. "And don't tell me nothing because I can hear it in your voice."

"There's a picture of me and Germain with Chris on the cover of the *National Enquirer,*" she managed to say through a fresh deluge of tears.

"What?"

"There's an article saying I was married to Germain the entire time I was married to Gunther. This has gone too far now. They've brought my children into this. Germain's so protective of Chris. He's going to hate me even more for this." Topaz got a box of tissues and blew her nose. "My life is a soap opera." She was crying again.

"Germain will understand. He knows the truth and he knows the information in that paper is a lie." Keisha tried to calm her down.

"But he'll be so upset when he finds out that he and Chris are on the cover of the *Enquirer*. He likes his privacy. This is between Gunther's family and me. They had no right to bring Chris into this. My son is going to think his mother is a real lowlife."

"People will do anything these days for a dollar. But Chris will love you no matter what. Germain's still in Sweden. This thing will be old news and they will have moved on to destroy someone else's life by the time he gets back."

"You spoke to Germain?" Topaz's tears quickly dissipated at the thought of seeing him.

"We're still playing phone tag. He's so hard to catch with that time difference, but he left me a message." Keisha whispered a silent prayer of thanks, sensing her friend was feeling better.

61

"What did he say?" Topaz was almost afraid to ask.

"Just that he was coming home next week and he couldn't wait to see me. Now I've got some drama for you to help me with." Keisha quickly changed the subject before they got into a long drawn-out conversation about Germain.

"You've got drama?" Topaz laughed. "How can I help?"

"Jade is coming over to spend the night while Sean's out of town. He asked me to keep an eye on her. Eric's away on a road trip, so I thought we could have a slumber party. You could bring Turquoise and I'll order some Thai food."

"Me spend the night with Jade? I want to help, Key, but I might kill the girl."

"If you don't come, I will kill her. She's a dead duck either way we go." Keisha laughed. "I promised Sean and there'll be two of us. Please . . . she's pregnant. Maybe she'll fall asleep."

"If I don't knock her out first." Topaz laughed. "I know, I'll get Nina to come, but she won't like her either."

"Yeah." Keisha laughed. "We'll give her to Nina."

Topaz watched her cousin walk in the door. "She just walked in. She never wants to do anything anymore. Let's hope I can talk her into it."

She hung up the phone while Nina quickly read the paper.

"You saw this?"

"Yes."

"And you're not out trying to kill somebody?" Nina's pretty face registered the shock.

"I was waiting for you." Topaz smiled.

"I knew it." She started toward the door she had just entered.

"Nina. I was just kidding. If I raise a big stink about that stupid article, I'll just draw more attention to myself."

Nina felt Topaz's forehead. "Are you feeling okay? Because you don't sound like the Topaz I know."

"I talked it over with Keisha. It'll be fine." Topaz smiled as she placed four bottles of champagne in a shopping bag.

"Keisha, I like her. She does wonders for you." Nina opened a container of strawberry yogurt. "I still have to meet her."

"She wants to meet you, too. She's having a slumber party at her house tonight for the girls. You're invited with me and Turquoise."

"A slumber party? I don't think so, Topaz. Maybe some other time."

"You never do anything with me anymore," Topaz wailed like a child. "If you aren't in school, you're in your room on that stupid computer or reading a book."

"All right, you're as bad as Jamil." Nina decided it would be simpler to give in, and she did want to meet the woman who was responsible for Topaz loosening her grip on her. "I'll come, but I'm taking my car so I can leave whenever I want."

"So where's the guest of honor?" Topaz glanced around the room looking for Jade.

"She called and said she was on her way three hours ago. I hope she's okay." A look of concern clouded Keisha's face.

"She's fine. Let's eat." Topaz had spotted all the cartons of Thai food in the kitchen. "I'm hungry."

Kendra came into the living room for Turquoise and her overnight bag. "Hi, Ni-Ni. Hello, Auntie Topaz."

"It's nice to see someone around here has manners." Nina made a face at Topaz and introduced herself to Keisha.

"I'm sorry. I forgot you two don't know each other."

"You'd forget your head if it wasn't screwed on." Nina left with the little girls and went into Kendra's room to see Barbie's Dream House while Keisha doubled over with laughter.

"Nina, it's such a pleasure to meet you." Keisha gave Topaz, who was already fixing herself a plate, an impish grin. "I can tell Nina and I are going to be great friends. We have a lot in common."

"Yeah, too much. I think I just made a big mistake."

Everyone was eating when Jade finally arrived. She got a major attitude the moment she spotted Topaz.

"I was painting and I kept promising myself I was going to stop and clean up, and before I knew it, three hours had gone by. I'm sorry I'm late," Jade finished, not really meaning it.

"I know what that's like. That's how I feel when I'm writing. I'm Nina. Topaz is my cousin." Nina smiled at Jade.

"Oh, you poor thing," Jade said. "We can pick our friends, but isn't it too bad we can't choose the members of our family?"

Keisha choked on her soda and Topaz reddened.

"Did she just say what I thought she said?" Topaz spoke loudly, but Nina had taken Jade into the kitchen for food so her comment went unheard.

"Didn't I see you put some Cristal in the fridge?" Keisha smiled at Topaz, who was still having a hard time with what Jade had just said.

"Yes, I'll get it." She stood up to go, but Keisha stopped her.

"No, I'll go. I think we could both use a drink right about now."

Keisha returned with a bottle of champagne and glasses. Topaz poured three glasses and handed one to Keisha and the other to her cousin.

"I'd like some too, please." Jade was so sweet, Topaz swore the girl was Dr. Jekyll and Mrs. Hyde.

"Are you supposed to drink while you're pregnant?" Only Nina was bold enough to ask the question and everyone waited to hear her response.

"My doctor said it was okay for me to have a glass once in a while." She accepted the glass Topaz poured and sipped it daintily while Topaz and Keisha exchanged glances.

"Lush," Topaz whispered under her breath and Keisha spat out her last sip and laughed. Topaz picked up Turquoise and sat her on her lap.

"She's adorable." Jade was still being friendly. "She looks just like you. How many children do you have?"

"Two. I have a son, eight, who lives with his father."

"I didn't pick you for the mother type. This is my first and last, and I can't wait until I have him so I can get back to work. I'm not cut out to be a housewife like Keisha."

Topaz poured more champagne in Keisha's glass before she could reply.

"What do you do?" Jade looked directly at Nina.

"I'm taking writing classes at UCLA Extension. And I'm the Hollywood correspondent for MTV. It's live or taped, depending on my story."

"That sounds so exciting. A real career woman." She looked at Topaz and Keisha. "I like that." Jade tapped her flute against Nina's.

"I work and I'm a mother," Topaz interjected.

"But you don't have a husband," Jade pointed out.

"And you need to mind your own damn business." Topaz glared at Jade, her amber eyes filled with venom.

Keisha set her glass of champagne on the table and looked at Jade. "You won't have a husband either if you don't start paying him a little more attention."

"That's a matter of opinion. I think you pay Eric too much attention. You need to get a life. A Laker wife . . . is that your claim to fame?"

Before Keisha had a chance to reply the little girls ran into the living room asking for ice cream and cookies.

"Y'all some vicious women," Nina whispered under her breath.

Topaz followed Keisha into the kitchen to get ice cream for the girls. "I'm going home before I kill her."

"Don't leave. You can't. I'll send her to bed. I promise."

"Send her ass to bed . . . quickly." Topaz was seething. "You'd better do something before I hurt her. I'm serious."

"I couldn't believe what she said to you. I couldn't let her talk like that to you in my home, but I shouldn't have lost my temper." Keisha licked a drop of strawberry ice cream from her finger.

"I wanted to hurt her for what she said to you. She's a bold little heifer. She just says whatever she likes." Topaz nibbled on a cookie.

"It must be the champagne." Keisha laughed as they went back into the living room.

"Jade, maybe you'd like to relax now." Keisha smiled at Topaz and then at Nina and Jade, who were seated together on the sofa eating ice cream. "It's been a long day and we're all a little tired, so I'll show you to your room."

"That sounds wonderful. I am a little tired from working in the studio. Nina, you're bunking with me, right?" Jade smiled at Nina, who looked at Topaz and Keisha.

"I hadn't intended to stay." Nina looked at Topaz, who pleaded with her eyes.

"Nina, please stay," Jade said. "It's Friday night and we can make popcorn. I want to hear all about MTV and your classes. I teach an art class at UCLA." Jade took her by the arm. "Keisha, show us to our room, please."

Keisha gave Nina pajamas while Topaz took the champagne into the bedroom.

"Can you believe that?" Keisha flopped onto the bed and drank the champagne Topaz had poured.

"That was strange. I almost feel sorry for bringing Nina, but I think Jade might like her." Topaz brushed her hair into a ponytail.

"And she hates us. I wonder why. I was beginning to think she was one of those women who can't get along with other women." Keisha clicked on the TV and got into bed.

"Like me?" Topaz laughed.

"Women have a problem with you. You've never had one with them." Keisha stared up at the ceiling while she spoke. "Jade definitely seemed to like Nina. But then she liked me at first, too. She was so sweet."

"And now she's a bitch. That's what I don't understand . . . why she doesn't like you. I'll get the scoop from Nina." Topaz lay in bed, silent, for several minutes. "Key, we haven't done this since we were in New York for my shoot, and I met Sean . . ."

"And I met my honey bunny." Keisha grinned. "In case I never said it, thanks for hooking a sister up."

"That's what friends are for. I never thought when we went out to dinner with those two fine brothers, you'd end up married to one. Say, maybe that's why she doesn't like me. Do you think Sean told her about us?"

"What's there to tell? You guys were only friends."

"Are Jade and Sean having problems?" Topaz was genuinely concerned.

"They're going through that adjustment period that all newlyweds go through, but Sean loves himself some Jade."

"She's lucky having someone to love her like that . . . and so are you. Did you ever think you'd be Eric's wife that night we met them?"

"I was a wishin' and a hopin' girl." Keisha giggled. "Did you think you'd be Germain's wife?"

"I knew I was going to marry that fine man, but I messed it up."

"Stop saying that."

"Well, I did."

"That's in the past. You've got to look ahead to what will be. God's going to fix this thing and it's going to be better than ever. You'll see."

Chapter Twelve

Nina picked up the first three chapters of her novel and smiled when she read her teacher's comments, sprawled across the top of the page next to the *A*.

Your writing shows great promise. Your characters are colorful, your descriptions vivid, and your story is engaging.

Nina tucked the pages into a folder inside her backpack and checked her watch. She still had several hours to kill before she was due at the studio for her taping, so she was going to sit in on Jade's art class.

She found the building and tiptoed inside the classroom. Students were sitting on stools in front of easels while Jade enlightened them on the use of color. Nina was fascinated as she watched Jade demonstrate various techniques. Her hands moved like magic across the paper, turning a few strokes of the brush into art.

She caught Nina's eye and smiled. Moments later, during the studio portion of the class, when they worked on their own creations, Jade sat down beside her and slipped off her shoes.

"I'm so glad you were able to come." She leaned over and gave her a hug. "What do you think of the class?" She smiled and her almond eyes became two slits.

"I think you got mad skills and I'm ready to go buy some paints and a pad."

"You're welcome to sit in on one of my classes anytime, Ms. Beaubien." She slowly pushed her feet into the designer flats that matched her outfit. She was a pretty, elegant young woman. Her long black hair was pulled back into a ponytail and bangs were bluntly cut across her forehead.

"You've got quite a load there." Nina held her hand out for support as Jade stood up.

"It's all those sweet potato pies and pound cakes Sean's mother sends. I'm as big as a house and the baby isn't due until May."

She waddled across the room inspecting each student's work and offering comments until the end of class. Afterward, they had lunch at Jade's favorite Japanese steak house in Westwood Village. She spoke in Japanese to the cook, ordering miso soup, salad, sushi, tempura, and steamed rice.

"He wanted to know if we were sisters." Jade poured steaming hot tea into their cups. "I told him we were. You don't mind, do you?"

Nina and Jade had stayed up all night at Keisha's talking. She liked Jade and was glad to have a friend besides her cousin and Jamil. Topaz's superstardom had changed her life forever. She always had to be careful of people trying to get close to Topaz through her. Nina knew Jade wasn't interested in her because of Topaz, and she was a celebrity herself because of her marriage to Sylk.

"I don't mind, and we do look something alike." Nina smiled. "I have a sister but we've never been very close. Topaz is like my sister."

"I still can't believe you're *her* cousin." Jade drank the last of her soup and picked up a slice of her spicy tuna roll with chopsticks and dipped it in soy sauce. "You're nothing alike. I would have lost it if you hadn't come to Keisha's."

"Really?" Nina was starting to feel uncomfortable and she wanted to change the subject. Topaz could be a handful, but she was still her cousin and best friend.

"Yes. My husband wants me to be friends with Keisha, but we don't have anything in common."

"Keisha's sweet." Nina bit into a piece of shrimp tempura.

"I guess, in a sickening sort of way." Jade laughed. "Let me stop because I'll have to go home and pray for forgiveness. Lord knows I've got enough things to work on already. Being married is enough to make you lose your religion. You think you've got it all together? Get married."

"I'm in no hurry to get married. I enjoy being single. Jamil gave me a ring and I still haven't given him an answer, but he's been real good about not pressuring me."

"Sometimes I wonder if Sean and I were married too soon. I love my husband but then sometimes I could kill him."

"Sean? He's so fine. I used to have the biggest crush on him. What's it like being married to him?"

Jade poured herself another cup of tea. "He's very sweet and sensitive and extremely romantic. Whenever he smiles I melt like butter."

"Like butter?" Nina laughed and Jade joined in.

"Like butter. Then he can be sloppy, leaves his clothes around, and that just irks me. He's a grown man and I am not his maid. He's a mama's boy. He thinks every woman should be like his mother and his family. . . . I don't know. Maybe I don't understand them. My family is so different. Everyone minds their own business. He talks to one of his brothers every day." She picked at a grain of rice with her chopsticks.

"It takes time for two people to gel. You love him, don't you?"

"With all my heart." Jade didn't even hesitate when she answered.

"See, that's the thing with Jamil. I don't know if I love him enough to spend the rest of my life with him."

"Well, if you have to ask, then you probably don't," Jade interjected quietly.

"That's what I've been thinking, but how do I know I'm not just scared and I really do love him enough to spend the rest of my life with him? How did you know Sean was the one?"

"I can't explain it, but I knew. I also knew I didn't want to spend the rest of my life without him."

"I can't live without him. . . . That's the best answer I've heard." Nina was genuinely excited.

"So do you know what you're going to do?" Jade felt the baby move and shifted her weight. "Be still, little boy, we'll have dessert later. And get off my bladder. Time to make a pit stop." She got up from the table.

The remains of lunch had been cleared when Jade returned, but the ladies continued talking.

"Do you know you're having a boy, or is that what you want?" Nina removed the wrapper from a piece of peppermint candy.

"I wanted to know. We've known that it was a boy as soon as we could tell from the ultrasound. Sean's mother had all boys so Sean wanted a girl."

"I'd like to interview you for my show."

"Really? Everyone always wants to talk about Sean when I do interviews. I'm my own person with my own identity."

"You're right, but he's a world-famous NBA star and people are curious about what it's like to be with him. You're the woman he sleeps with."

"He's the man I sleep with." Jade laughed. "And it's all good."

"I hear you, girlfriend." They slapped a high five, and then Jade became very serious.

"Did *she* have anything going on with my husband?"

"Who?" Nina was no longer laughing.

"*Her* . . . your cousin."

"Topaz?"

"Yes." Jade folded her arms and looked at Nina.

So that's why she doesn't like Topaz.

"They were friends, but they never really dated." Nina was surprised that Jade was actually jealous of Topaz.

71

"She was with him the first time I met him at the museum."

"They were friends. Topaz is still in love with her first husband, Germain. She'd do anything to have him back in her life. He's her one true love. She doesn't even date."

"Really?" Jade looked relieved. "I hope she gets him back, then. . . . I want to go to the studio with you. Are you interviewing anyone famous today? But we should go get our hair cut first. I've been wanting to do something different. Sean will have a cow, but I don't care." She stood up and took Nina by the arm.

This girl changes her mind with the drop of a hat. Talk about mood swings . . . it must be the pregnancy. I swear I'm never getting pregnant. Jamil's never touching me again.

"I'm doing *The Hype* today. It's a gossip segment. I'll let you know when I do something fun. Don't you think you should go home and spend some time with your husband, Mrs. Ross? And you did promise the baby some ice cream."

The light faded from Jade's countenance when Nina mentioned going home, but it returned to her face when she mentioned ice cream for the baby.

"Nina, you are so much fun." She hugged her and kissed her on the cheek. "I'll call you later."

She seems lonely.

Nina thought about Jade for the rest of the evening.

"Topaz, do you know if anyone's planned a shower for Jade?" Nina was reading to Turquoise, and Topaz lay next to her listening.

"I don't know. Who cares?"

"I do." Nina spoke softly so she wouldn't wake the baby.

"Don't tell me you were hanging out with *her*." Topaz's face registered her displeasure.

They're just alike, Nina realized. *Two divas with tremendous egos. Does Sean know how pick 'em or what?*

"I want to give her a shower."

"Why?"

"Because she's my friend." Nina gave Topaz a look that told her the subject was not open for discussion.

"Whatever . . . but you can't give it here."

"I don't want to have it here. I'll ask Keisha, she'll help me."

"No, she won't. She hates the girl, too."

Nina ignored her and phoned Keisha, who readily agreed.

"We can have it at my house," Keisha offered generously. "I'm glad you mentioned it because I wasn't thinking."

Nina smiled as she hung up the phone. Jade was going to have a fabulous baby shower. She glanced at Topaz, who hadn't said one word, but Nina knew she had heard her conversation with Keisha.

For some reason, Nina was determined to be Jade's friend. Jade needed her . . . and if Topaz didn't like it, that only sweetened the pot by keeping her focused on her goal . . . to keep her life separate from her cousin's.

Chapter Thirteen

Keisha sat in a soul food restaurant sipping an icy glass of lemonade. It felt like summer and it was barely spring. Mindlessly, she wrote with the tip of her fingernail in the moisture that had collected on the outside of the jelly jar.

"Hey, gorgeous. Can a brother get some love?" Twinkling hazel eyes smiled at her from a handsome, or as most would say, a pretty café au lait face.

"Germain!" Keisha leaped from her chair and dove into his arms. "You look so good."

He did look good, dressed in an expensive designer suit. The women in the restaurant couldn't stop staring. He laughed, gave her another hug, and pulled out the chair across from her.

"Dang, man, if I wasn't a married woman."

"I don't want to die. That big, tall man you're married to will never kick my behind."

"Eric likes you." Keisha laughed.

"And I intend to keep it that way. I like living." He carefully placed his jacket on the chair next to him. "My home girl livin' like a superstar in Los Angeles. What's up?"

They grinned at each other while a waitress took a double order for smothered steak and rice, yams, collard greens, and potato salad.

"This is pretty good," Germain commented halfway through the meal. "But nothin' like the way we do it in Atlanta, GA. You be throwin' down like this for Eric?" His southern drawl was as charming as ever.

"Sometimes, but he's on a special diet so we have a personal chef during the season."

"I hear you. I have a woman who picks Chris up from school, gets him started on his homework, and makes dinner. She lives with us, too."

"A nanny?" Keisha stopped chewing and looked up at him.

"Yeah, a nanny. I just hate that word. It just sounds so stuck-up . . . you know."

Keisha smiled at Germain's modesty.

"I try to be home by dinner every night so we can talk and go over his homework. It gets hard sometimes but we manage. He's in Atlanta for a few weeks with the family. I miss him. Thank you, ma'am."

A waitress refilled their glasses with lemonade and Keisha had to smile when she heard the all too familiar southern courtesy he extended.

"Dr. Gradney, you will always be a charming southern boy. I bet you have women standing in line. That waitress can't stay away from our table and every female in here is drooling."

"Stop it, Key." He was actually blushing.

"So how are you doing with the ladies? Anybody special?"

He dug his spoon into a dish of banana pudding that the waitress had been ever so kind to warm for him. "I've been seeing someone but it's nothing serious."

Keisha sighed with relief and wondered how she could work Topaz into the conversation without being too obvious.

"So how do you like it here, Mrs. Johnson? I'm sure you've been exposed to the best of everything by the Laker organization."

"To be honest, I didn't want to come and I didn't really like it at first, but now I do. I have friends and I love the weather, especially when it's like this."

"So you kickin' it with some of the other players' wives?" Germain finished the last bite of his dessert and the waitress quickly cleared away his dish.

"No, I've been hanging out with Topaz."

"Topaz?" Germain was shocked. You're hanging out with *her?*"

Gotcha . . . you still care. She smiled and quickly nodded her head to agree.

"She's so Hollywood and you're not. What do you have in common?" He searched her face, eager for a response.

"I beg your pardon, but I am the wife of a Laker, Dr. Gradney, and this is Hollywood."

"Aw, Key, you know what I mean. You could have married Michael Jordan and you wouldn't change, but Topaz did. She's caught up into all this star stuff."

"Not anymore. She's changed, Germain. She really has. I was amazed."

"So what's so different?" He settled back in his chair, ready to hear the story.

"She grew up. She's really into her daughter. She has the prettiest little girl. Turquoise looks just like her, same golden eyes . . . Topaz with a tan." She noticed a hint of a smile on Germain's face.

"She takes her everywhere. She even kept my daughter so Eric and I could go out. She's toned down. She's still working on her career, but she's different . . . better."

"Interesting."

She could tell Germain was thinking so she decided to go for the jugular. She and Karla had been praying about this meeting for weeks. "I'm giving a dinner party. You remember our friends, Sean and Jade?"

"Yes."

"Sean's brother, Kirk, and his wife, Karla, our friends from New York, are flying in. You remember them?"

"Yeah, one of those crazy twins. I could never forget them. Which one is the wild one?"

"That's Kyle." Keisha laughed. "He's not able to come."

"Too bad. That boy is crazy. I'll never forget the night he danced on his brother's table and it broke. I almost wet my pants."

"This party will be somewhat calmer." Keisha laughed. "Nobody's dancing on my new furniture. Nina is Topaz's cousin."

"I remember Nina, the beautiful chocolate girl with all that long hair. I really liked her."

"Nina is sweet, and smart, too. She's coming with her boyfriend . . . and then you and Topaz," she added softly. "It won't be like a date and then you could see for yourself how she's changed. You could bring Chris, too."

"Okay, Key, count me in. I've got to get back to the office." He paid for lunch, kissed her, and zipped away in a convertible Porsche.

And he said Topaz was Hollywood. You're not doing too bad yourself with your nanny. She laughed as she dialed Topaz's cell.

"Guess who's coming to dinner," Keisha sang into the phone.

"Who?" She could hear music in the background so she knew Topaz was still at the studio.

"You and Germain and a few other people."

"You saw Germain?"

"We just had lunch. Girl, the brother was so fine I wish I could have e-mailed him to you."

Topaz screamed and Keisha laughed. "Girl, you're crazy. You saw my man." She panted into the phone.

"It's in the bag. You just show up looking fine."

It was Keisha's first dinner party in LA and everything had to be perfect . . . for so many reasons. When she was late leaving her hair appointment because her stylist wanted to touch up her highlights, she had promised herself she wouldn't get nervous. There was a line when she stopped to pick up the dry cleaning, another line at the market, and she still had food to prepare.

She had followed Germain's cue and prepared a southern menu, cooking many of the dishes days ahead of time. All she had to do was fry the chicken that was already cut up and seasoned, and put the macaroni and cheese casserole in the oven.

Karla called from Jade's, wanting to talk, and she was still dressed by seven. Keisha was serving a candlelight buffet in the dining room. She was helping her maid arrange the chafing dishes when the telephone rang. She sucked in her breath when she heard his voice.

"Key . . . I'm sorry but there's been a change in plans."

"What is it, Germain?" She sank down on the sofa, feeling as though the wind had been knocked out of her.

"Chris has a big school project he has to finish by tomorrow. . . ."

"You're not coming?" She was almost in tears.

"I'm still coming, but . . ."

I don't like that but. She prepared herself for the bomb she knew he was about to drop.

"I'm bringing a date," he finished quietly.

"Okay, Germain. We'll see you when you get here." She hung up the phone and was sitting there staring at it when Eric walked into the room looking like new money.

"What's wrong, baby?"

"Germain's bringing a date. I'd better call Topaz."

"Yeah, you'd better. I don't want to see a brother get shot up in here." He was trying not to laugh, but she did.

"Eric." She threw a pillow at him and dialed Topaz's number.

"T, honey, I'm glad I caught you. Are you sitting down?"

"What is it, Keisha? You're scaring me."

"Germain just called. He's bringing a date."

There was a long silence before she replied. "So. I'll just have to bring one, too."

Keisha hung up and grinned. *That's my girl.*

The Rosses arrived first. It was the first time Sean, Kirk, and Eric had all been together since the opening of the gallery, and the party was definitely started. Nina and Jamil arrived next, followed by Germain and Sherry, a classy and obviously professional woman. Keisha couldn't help noticing that she lacked Topaz's beauty and flash. Topaz had always been a showstopper, while this woman might get lost in a crowd. Everyone faded into the background when Topaz was around.

They were eating Keisha's famous crab cakes and drinking sparkling cider when the doorbell rang. Keisha almost ran to the door, eager for the showdown to begin. Topaz stepped in with her blond mane blown silky straight. She was wearing her favorite fur, the one that matched her hair, and a little black dress with spaghetti straps.

"This is my friend, Pete Wingate."

Keisha wanted to scream "You go, girl" when she saw the tall, extremely handsome blond, with cobalt-blue eyes. She took them in the living room and made introductions. For a minute, everyone was silent. She knew Topaz had planned on making a grand entrance.

Keisha looked at Germain, who was trying hard to act as though he weren't bothered, but his handsome face lacked its usual color. The moment Topaz spotted his date, Keisha saw the green-eyed monster cloud her friend's sparkling amber eyes.

Eric greeted Topaz, then Sean, who made a fuss and kissed her on the cheek. Topaz kissed Jade, who immediately left for more crab cakes, then Nina and Jamil. Finally, she and Pete stood opposite Germain and Sherry.

"Hello, Germain. This is Peter Wingate." Topaz smiled prettily while Germain looked Pete up and down.

"Hello, Topaz. This is Dr. Sherry Hobbs. Nice seeing you." He took the woman by the arm and escorted her over to the bar for another drink.

"We'd better serve dinner now," Eric suggested. "I'll go hide the knives before somebody gets cut."

No one seemed to notice how quiet Topaz was except Keisha and Nina. They were having dessert when Keisha finally had a chance to speak with her privately.

"You okay, T?" She brushed a lock of hair from her face.

"He barely said two words to me all night. He still hates me." She couldn't conceal the pain on her pretty face.

Germain walked up to Keisha as soon as she went back into the living room.

"Key, this was nice, but we've got to go. We both have early days."

"I understand." She kissed him and handed him a plate of food to take home to Chris.

"You're the best, Key."

When she returned from seeing Germain and Sherry out, Sean was talking to Topaz.

"It'll be okay, you just keep the faith. He'll come around. He'd be a fool not to."

"Thanks, Sean." Topaz managed one of her prettiest smiles, but Keisha knew she was hurting.

"Don't listen to him," Jade interjected. "If you're smart you'll move on, because that man made it quite obvious he no longer cares."

Chapter Fourteen

Jade moved as swiftly as she could down the side of the bike path as it curved around the marina toward the water. She passed colorful sailboats, cabin cruisers, and yachts floating in the harbor.

"From behind, no one would ever know you're pregnant." Nina couldn't stop teasing. "I'll spot you fifty yards."

Jade trotted on and seconds later she heard Nina's nylon sweatpants swishing beside her. "Baby, you so fine. Can I, like, get with you?" She spoke in a deep streetwise voice and managed not to chuckle.

Jade immediately stopped moving, leaned against a light pole, and giggled. "You cheated. You're not supposed to make me laugh."

Both of them sat down on a black wrought-iron bench and laughed until they cried.

"I hate you," Jade finally said. "I feel so fat and ugly and you're all fine and toned with that diamond in your navel. Don't ever have a baby. You'll ruin your cute little shape. Your back hurts, your feet swell. You just get ugly."

"You are not ugly, but I'm not having anyone's baby. When we get you back in shape, I'll take you to get your navel pierced. Sean would love it."

"I don't know about that. He doesn't want me changing anything. He hated my hair."

Nina ran her hand through the black shiny hair that had been cut in short layers and trimmed to her neck. Every strand of the precision cut fell back into place. "It's so cute, but you did cut all of your hair off. I'm sure it's easy to take care of. How could he not like it?"

"I thought he was going to croak. My husband is so old-fashioned. He likes what he likes, but I don't care. It was my hair and he didn't have to wash it. It's so easy now. It takes fifteen minutes to blow-dry or I can just put some gel on it."

"He just has to get used to it. Your son is going to come out looking like Rapunzel."

"Whatever. I'll just be glad when my baby comes out."

"You're crazy." Nina laughed and extended a hand. Come on, Big Mama, let's go home."

They chatted all the way back to the Tower.

"Sean's brother, Kirk, is fine," Nina sang. He has a twin?"

"Kyle." Jade slowed her stride and Nina fell in with her.

"Your sister-in-law, Karla, is so cool. Why are they staying at Keisha's house and not with you?"

"They were best friends or something back in New Jersey, and they're both boring housewives who spend all their time in Bible studies and catering to their men and children."

"Kyrie is too precious. She adores her Uncle Sean. No wonder he wanted a little girl."

Jade only grunted and Nina didn't know if her friend didn't feel well or if she had treaded into a sensitive area by mentioning her in-laws, so they finished their walk in silence.

Nina showered in the guest bath and was sitting in the family room reading a magazine when Jade finally emerged freshly showered and smiling.

"I'm ready to get out of here. Let's get something to eat. I'm starvin' like Marvin." Jade grinned. "Let's go have some sushi."

"Okay." Nina stood up and tossed the magazine on the table. "Are you sure you're up to it? We can order in."

"I feel fine. I just needed to relax in a warm bath. We're getting out of here. Sean, Eric, and Kirk will be here soon. I'll leave them some menus so they can order in."

They left in Nina's truck. When she headed out of the Marina toward Ladera Heights, Jade looked at her.

"Where are we going?"

"I need to stop by Keisha's for a minute." Jade groaned as Nina stopped in front of the house and pulled her out of the car.

"Come on, Big Mama. You're coming in, too. It wouldn't be right if Keisha looked out here and saw you sitting in the car. And I promised Sean I wouldn't let you out of my sight. He's much too fine to argue with."

Jade sat there looking at her as if she were crazy.

"We'll only be here a minute," Nina coaxed.

"One quick minute."

Keisha greeted them both with a hug. "Come on in, you guys. Nina, the papers you need are in here."

She led them inside to the dining room, where they were greeted with a chorus of "surprise" from Keisha, Topaz, Karla, and Jade's assistants, Akiba and Kiyoko.

"Oh, my God. You guys must want me to have the baby now. What is all this?"

"It's your baby shower, silly." Nina smiled. "Surprise."

Jade looked around the room utterly amazed. There was a green and silver banner draped across the room that said IT'S A BOY, and an exquisite tea with an assortment of appetizers, finger sandwiches, scones, and petit fours with the palest mint green frosting. The ladies had outdone themselves.

"You knew about this all the time, didn't you?" Jade looked at Nina.

"Of course she did," Topaz offered. "My cousin is the ultimate party planner."

After the tea and games, it was time for presents . . . a big basket of accessories for a newborn baby boy from her assistants, the most adorable outfits and a car seat from Keisha, a stroller from Karla, and an engraved sterling silver spoon from Nina. Topaz insisted that her gift be opened last.

"I know this is a baby shower, but my gift is for the mother." Topaz smiled as they watched Jade unwrap an ensemble of Victoria's Secret lingerie, a sexy red nightgown, edible body gels, a bottle of Cristal, and two baccarat flutes. Every woman in the room screamed, Jade the loudest of all.

"So you can get your swerve on properly," Topaz squealed. "And with that fine man, it won't be hard." They continued screaming as Jade jumped up and danced with the nightgown and Nina snapped pictures. Surprisingly, she broke into tears moments later, and they all looked at one another, amazed.

"What's wrong, honey?" Nina kneeled on the floor in front of her while Keisha gently massaged her back. Jade's only response was a deluge of tears. Finally, through a series of sobs, she offered an explanation.

"No one has ever been this nice to me before. No one liked me because I'm biracial. Black girls were always mean to me and called me a chink and the Japanese girls were just as nasty and called me a nigger."

From somewhere she found more tears to cry. Keisha handed a box of tissues to Nina, who wiped her friend's tears. Karla sat on the floor next to Nina and began to talk to Jade.

"God is healing you. People have hated your beauty and you thought they hated you. You have sought your validation from your work because you don't believe you are beautiful. You are a beautiful woman, Jade, and you will realize this when you begin to cultivate your inner beauty by developing your spirit."

Chapter Fifteen

Topaz dug in her purse for her compact and fussed with her hair. "I'm so depressed, Keisha. I still can't believe Germain had the nerve to show up at your dinner party with that woman and he wouldn't even talk to me. He's never going to forgive me."

Keisha took her eyes off the road momentarily and glanced at Topaz, who quickly brushed away a tear.

"And now I have to go to court and deal with Gunther's crazy family. I get depressed every time I have to come here."

Keisha parked and they walked slowly up to the courthouse.

"Oh, my God, Keisha, we'll never make it inside."

A small throng of photographers and cameramen were gathered in front of the building and the moment they spotted Topaz, they rushed toward her, thrusting mikes and cameras in her face. Several husky security guards, who looked more like Secret Service men, pushed the vultures aside and rushed the ladies into the building where Topaz's attorneys were waiting.

"Things have spun out of control with the press since Ms. Martinez's appearance in *Playboy*. You're on the cover of just about every tabloid. You shouldn't have come here by yourself, Topaz." Her lead counsel issued the warning. "Please take the necessary precautions for your own safety and bring security for all future sessions, Ms. Black."

Topaz groaned and made a face. "I'm only trying to have a life. I didn't think it would be this bad."

She spotted Gunther's sister, Rosalyn, with Carmen, and her son, Gunther Jr., as the men led them into the courtroom.

"Look." Topaz quickly pointed them out to Keisha. "I can't believe the hoochie brought the baby to court. She's really milking this thing for all she can get. I wonder if someone told her to bring the baby."

"Probably," Keisha whispered before she sat down behind Topaz. "I'm sure he didn't ask to come."

Light to heavy bantering went back and forth among counsel with a series of motions for continuance filed. With no resolution in sight, the court was adjourned once the judge announced the date of their next hearing.

"Will this madness ever end?" Topaz muttered as they were ushered out.

Lightbulbs flashed and TV cameras lit up the hallway as Topaz and Keisha emerged, wearing sunglasses and poker faces.

"I don't remember getting this much press when my CD sold over ten million copies," she whispered as they ducked inside the ladies' rest room for cover.

"Yes, but this is about Gunther's millions and that fine house in Bel Air."

"They'll never see a dime or set foot in my house," Topaz sneered.

The security guards positioned themselves like guard dogs in front of the door so no one was permitted to enter while the feeding frenzy slowly dispersed. To their surprise, Rosalyn, Carmen, and Gunther Jr. were also in the rest room.

"Hello, Topaz. How are you and how's my niece?"

Topaz ignored her completely and fussed with her hair in the mirror. Rosalyn's resemblance to her late husband was uncanny at times.

"We were fine until all of this. I can't believe you want to know. It was because of you that I'm here and my children and I are all over the press." She turned to walk out of the door just as quickly as she had come in, when she felt Keisha's hand on her arm.

"Rosalyn. I'm Keisha. Topaz and I grew up together in Atlanta." Keisha smiled and Topaz looked at her as if she were crazy.

"You're Eric Johnson's wife." Rosalyn returned the smile and shook Keisha's hand while Topaz wondered if both of them had lost their minds.

"That's me." Keisha smiled at Carmen.

"I watched Eric play in New York. I'm glad he's a Laker now." Rosalyn relaxed and leaned against the tile wall. Little Gunther sat on the floor and Carmen scooped him up.

"I'm glad he's here, too. I didn't think I'd like LA, but it's like old times being here with my girl."

"Keisha, we really need to go now. You know I have that other appointment."

Keisha looked at Topaz, whose eyes were amber daggers, and told her with her eyes to chill. She looked at the little boy in his mother's arms, who was watching her every move.

"Hi, sweetie. What's your name?"

"Gunther." He looked at her with eyes as big as saucers.

"You are so cute. Can I hold you?" She extended her arms to the child and Camen looked at Rosalyn, who nodded her approval while Topaz sighed loudly.

"He doesn't like strangers." Carmen smoothed a lock of his hair with slender fingers with brightly polished nails.

"I'm no stranger. I'm Keisha." Everyone was surprised when he reached for Keisha, who took the little boy and balanced him on her hip. He reached up to touch the pattern in her hammered gold necklace.

"You like pretty things, huh? A man with taste. Come here, Topaz." Keisha pulled her next to her. "Say hi to this lady. Her name is Topaz."

"Hello." Gunther Jr. looked directly at Topaz and then at Keisha. "You're pretty."

"Flattery will get you everything." Keisha found a piece of candy in her purse and handed it to him.

"You're pretty, too." He looked at Topaz. "I saw you on TV. You're my sister's mommy. Can she come over and play?" His English was amazing.

Topaz looked at Rosalyn and Carmen and sighed even louder as she gave Keisha a "what have you gotten me into?" look.

"I have a little girl, too. Maybe you can all play together," Keisha answered before things had a chance to become more uncomfortable.

"That would be nice." Rosalyn produced a business card and jotted down a number on the back. "This is home and work. Maybe we can arrange something soon."

Keisha took the card and handed Gunther back to his mother. "Bye, handsome."

She followed Topaz out of the rest room. The corridor was clear except for a few people en route to various courtrooms. Topaz was silent as the security guards followed them out to Keisha's Lexus.

"Why did you do that?" Topaz exploded once they were in the car. "I'm in the middle of a lawsuit and you practically invited them over for milk and cookies."

"That's your daughter's family and all this drama is ridiculous. Gunther Jr. is Turquoise's brother. They proved his paternity, so settle this thing. That little boy had nothing to do with what went on between you, Gunther, and his mother."

Topaz's eyes blazed with anger. "I can't believe you're taking that hoochie's side. You know she got pregnant on purpose."

"Whatever. . . . That little boy has no father. I'm not taking anyone's side. Settle this thing. Get out of the press and get on with your life. All this drama isn't doing anyone any good."

*　*　*

Topaz was silent all the way to the restaurant. Keisha's words made plenty of sense. The only ones who ever really won legal battles were the attorneys because of their exorbitant fees.

"I'd like a bottle of Cristal," Topaz told the waiter as soon as they were seated.

"Excuse me, but we're not ready to order anything yet," Keisha cut in. "We'll let you know when we're ready."

Topaz was speechless as Keisha leaned in to whisper, "Why are you ordering champagne? I see nothing to celebrate. You're using it to cover your pain."

Topaz's mouth dropped open and then she closed it as the tears welled up in her eyes. "I was wishing for some coke and I haven't touched the stuff in years," she mumbled as she dug in her bag for a tissue. "The last time I did any was the day I married Gunther."

Tears streamed out of her eyes as she frantically searched for a tissue. She dabbed at her eyes with a linen napkin.

"What's the matter, T?" Keisha handed her a Kleenex. "This doesn't have anything to do with Carmen or the baby, does it?"

She shook her head no as the tears flowed. Their waiter appeared and Keisha sent him away. "I never loved Gunther the way I loved Germain."

"What is it, then?"

"Germain." She sobbed. "He doesn't want me."

Keisha handed her several more tissues.

"I miss him so much and I'm lonely." She was really broken up. She had put up a good front since the night of the dinner, and that coupled with Gunther's family and the lawsuit were too much for her to handle. She had done a good job of masking her pain with alcohol until Keisha snagged her.

"Have you ever prayed about Germain?"

Topaz looked up, somewhat amazed by her question. It had never crossed her mind.

"No," Keisha answered for her. "We're getting our food to go so we can really talk."

* * *

At Topaz's house, Keisha took the pastas and caesar salad out of the cartons and fixed their plates, but Topaz barely touched her food.

"I was hoping Germain would call me and he hasn't."

"He'll call."

"When?" She was practically crying again. "When my breasts are down to my knees and I'm bald?"

Keisha tried not to laugh because she knew Topaz was serious. "I don't think you'll ever let that happen."

"So when?"

"I don't know. And don't start feeling sorry for yourself. You've already had enough pity parties. There's a marriage class at church and you and I are going."

"Marriage class?" The idea of attending a class on marriage was foreign to her.

"Marriage enrichment. It's a class where people talk about their relationships, any problems they may be having, and various solutions."

"You talk about those kind of things in church?"

"Yes. When you get hired for a job you receive training. No one teaches you how to be a wife or a husband. Getting married doesn't make you an expert on marriage."

"I never really thought about it like that, but that's true." Topaz was silent for several moments.

"Don't you want to be ready when God does put the two of you back together?"

"All right," Topaz agreed, brightening. "I'll go. I'll do whatever it takes to get my man back and be the kind of wife Germain needs."

"You're gonna be just fine, T." Keisha smiled at her friend, but a frown clouded Topaz's pretty face.

"Germain and I should never have gotten married, huh?" She pushed her plate, still full, aside and looked to Keisha for more answers.

"You two had something most people never have . . . love. But I think you guys should have waited. You both had dreams, but you got pregnant and wanted to do the right thing for your baby."

"Yeah, I did, except I didn't try hard enough. I took Germain for granted. I thought he'd always love me and always be there."

"Have you ever apologized?" Keisha pushed her empty plate aside.

"That day at the clinic." She spoke softly as she traced an invisible spot on the granite counter.

"Have you tried again?"

"No. I never saw him again until the night of your party."

"Why don't you write him a letter and tell him how you feel?"

"A letter . . . That's a good idea, Key. You know how he reads everything." She looked up at her friend and smiled.

"And pray that God sends him back. You do everything you can do, then God does His part."

"You're really serious about God, huh?"

"I couldn't make it without Him." Keisha cleared the table and took their plates to the sink.

It had been some day and Keisha had gotten her through it. Topaz watched her remove the dishes and looked at her as though she were seeing her for the first time. All sorts of thoughts bombarded her mind and her head was spinning. For the first time in years, she really believed she could have a relationship with Germain again, and she was excited.

Chapter Sixteen

Nina looked at the three folders lying on her desk that held her script, chapters for the novel, and ideas for upcoming news stories for MTV, contemplating what to work on first. She had finished her classes and the MTV tapings for the week. It was Thursday, the beginning of her weekend, when she always tried to sequester herself from the rest of the world and write until Monday morning.

She was usually unsuccessful, but with Jamil in New York and Topaz somewhere with Keisha, the outlook was favorable. Jade, at home, hopefully with her feet up, had Sean to cater to her whims, leaving Nina free to write to her heart's desire with no interruptions.

She reached into the bottom of her nightstand and pulled out a shiny red metal lockbox. The tiny key, located on the ring with the others, unlocked her treasure chest. She took the box and went out on her balcony that overlooked the sprawling green grass on the estate, which had been freshly cut that morning. It was a warm, overcast day that hinted of summer.

Nina opened the box and carefully inspected its contents: approximately five hundred dollars in cash, Jamil's engagement ring, still in the case, and a small plastic bag that contained her stash of weed. She pulled out a joint and lit it. She hadn't touched a speck of cocaine since Gunther's death, but she still liked to smoke. It was organic, an herb, she had convinced herself.

She opened the case and looked at the engagement ring and tried it on her finger. It was a beautiful ring but she wasn't ready to get married. Every time she tried to bring up the subject for discussion, Jamil told her that she was his woman and when she was ready they would get married. She took the ring off, placed it back in the case, and put the case back in the box. She still remembered Jade's advice . . . *Don't marry him if you can live without him.* Who was she fooling? She *could* live without Jamil.

She carefully put out her joint and placed the remainder in the box and carried it back inside her room. She saw her folders and flipped through ideas for stories. There was an invitation to a party at the House of Blues for the release of Kobe Bryant's CD. She was going to do a story on him and that fine Robert Horry from the Lakers. She had sold her first story on Jamil to *Vibe.* Her writing career had really started to blossom and she was establishing an identity for herself apart from Topaz.

Jade had finally consented to an interview as well, after the baby was born. Nina had promised to tell Jade's story, unlike the other interviews that ended up focusing on Sean. But there was no way she was going to be on television with that big belly. Nina thought about her friend and laughed. Jade was a piece of work.

She made some notes in the file and opted to work on the screenplay, a romantic comedy. She had finished the first act, the hardest part. She really wanted to work on her favorite project, the novel. She could write for hours and it seemed like minutes. She had long completed the required writing for her class, but she wanted to finish it so she could sell it. She was writing about a singer. She knew everyone would think it was Topaz, but she didn't care. Her life was so intertwined with her cousin's that it was her story anyway.

She heard voices downstairs and quickly slid the lockbox back into her nightstand. Topaz was home. Minutes later, she appeared in Nina's doorway loaded down with shopping bags.

"I'm writing, Topaz. I'll come see what you bought later." She hoped there were no telltale signs of the pungent herb in her room.

"You never spend time with me anymore. You just hang out with Jade. But that's cool with me." Like a disappointed child, Topaz started toward the hallway that connected the east and west wings of the house. "I just thought you might want to see what I bought for you."

"You shopped for me?"

"Yes." Topaz's eyes sparkled with excitement.

"Get back in here." Nina pulled her into the room and relieved her of some of the bags. "What did you buy?"

Topaz shuffled through various bags, producing a pair of black leather pants, a couple of sweaters, and a pair of boots.

Nina squealed with delight. "Can I hire you to be my stylist?" She immediately slipped off her sweats and tried on the leather pants, which fit her like a glove. "You got skills, girl."

"That's me, Topaz, born to shop." She sat on the floor and sifted through the remaining bags while Nina tried on one of the sweaters. "I got you something else. I hope I didn't leave them in the car." She looked in another bag and pulled out a pair of metallic gold and black snakeskin pants. "Here they are." She held up the pants for Nina to see.

"You always get the best stuff." She grabbed the pants and tried them on. "Did I mention that I love you?"

"Sure, you do. I bet Jade doesn't shop for you."

"You're right about that." Nina twisted in the mirror so she could see her behind. "Does my butt look too big?"

"No." Topaz stretched out on her bed. "Brothers like a sister with junk in her trunk."

"You sound like Jamil." Nina laughed.

"You look good. We just need to do something with that hair."

"What's wrong with my hair?" Nina turned around, demanding an answer.

"Nothing . . . except you're MTV now and you still look like a Valley Girl." Topaz laughed.

"I do not." Nina played with her hair in the mirror. "Where's my Turkey?"

"Stop calling my baby Turkey. I let her spend the night with Keisha and Kendra. There was some special program for the kids at her church tonight. I want to do your hair."

"What do you want to do to my hair?" Nina thought she had changed the subject from her hair, but Topaz was right back on it.

"Cut it." Topaz got a comb and ran it through her cousin's long black hair.

"Cut it? I don't think so." She backed away from Topaz as the phone rang.

"I'm not letting you answer that." Topaz jumped on Nina's back and they both fell on the bed and laughed.

"You're crazy." Nina laughed as her cell phone rang.

"Someone's really trying to get you. It must be Jamil, calling to check on his woman."

The phone rang again and Topaz answered it.

"It's Jade," she told Nina several moments later. "Why are you whispering?" she said into the phone.

"Because I just had a contraction," Jade said. "I'm at the studio and I can't find Sean. Ask Nina if she will come get me and take me to the hospital."

"How far apart are your contractions?" Topaz was very concerned.

"About every thirty minutes. I think they started this morning, but I wasn't sure until they started getting worse and now I can't find Sean." Her whispers turned into sobs.

"Okay. You're fine. You're just having a baby. We're on our way. Do your breathing. We'll call you from the cell as soon as we get in the car."

"Thanks, Topaz," Nina said. She changed back into her sweats and got her purse. "Will you come to the hospital with us?"

"Sure. I remember when I had Chris. I was scared. I was at home by myself and Germain was at school. I paged him and he came right home and took me to the hospital."

"I wonder where Sean is, and what the hell is she doing in the studio? She is such a brick head." Nina frowned as she spoke.

Topaz talked to Jade while Nina drove. "We're right outside and coming in to get you."

Jade held on to both their arms as she hobbled out to the car. She had another contraction as she got into the truck and practically squeezed the life out of Topaz's hand. Topaz got into the back with her.

"Okay, breathe, Jade, breathe." Topaz began the breathing exercises while Jade screamed.

"Don't you know how to do the breathing?" Nina watched them from the rearview mirror.

"No." She was whispering again.

"Didn't you go to the classes?" Topaz demanded.

"No. I was out of town." She cried as the tears flowed.

"It's okay. Stop crying and breathe." Topaz demonstrated the technique again.

"You are such a brick head," Nina fussed. "And don't be having no babies in my Rover."

"Some friend you are." Jade stopped crying to laugh. "My water already broke."

"And you were at the studio? What's Sean's number?" Topaz took out her cell phone.

"Use mine. We have the walkie-talkie kind." Topaz called Sean several times but there was no answer. Nina dropped them at the ER and went to park the truck. Jade and Topaz were taken into a prep room, where Jade started to cry again.

"Sean, Sean. I want Sean. Where is my boo?" She curled up in the bed and cried like a little girl. Nina walked in and looked at Topaz.

"How is she?"

"Do you know where Sean is?" Topaz asked Nina.

"He went to play basketball with Eric."

"I hate basketball," Jade managed through her tears.

"Can they give her anything?" Nina smoothed Jade's hair.

"It's too soon. She still needs to dilate a few more centimeters," Topaz explained.

"I am so glad you're here because I wouldn't know what the hell I'm doing." Nina sat down and tried Sean again on the phone. "I don't remember it being like this with you . . . and I was going to have a nice quiet weekend." Nina looked almost as bad as Jade.

Topaz got Jade some ice chips and Nina a Coke and they both seemed to calm down for a few minutes. When Jade's contractions increased to every fifteen minutes, a nurse finally gave her something for the pain.

"I am never having a baby," Nina vowed, looking at Jade.

"It's not all that bad. It hurts like hell, but it's worth it." Topaz smiled.

"Sean, Sean . . . where are you, Sean? How are you guys related?" She was crying one minute and talking the next.

"Our mothers are sisters," Nina explained.

"You don't look alike except you're both pretty. Can I be your cousin, too?" The drug had started to work.

"Sure you can, babe. But I thought we were sisters?" Nina wiped Jade's forehead with a cloth.

"That's right, we are. So Topaz is my cousin, too, now."

It was finally time for Jade to go into the delivery room. Sean and Eric arrived just as they were about to take her inside.

"Where were you when I needed you?" Jade cried as another contraction hit.

"I'm sorry, baby. We were playing basketball and I put my phone in the bag. I couldn't hear it, but I should have checked in." He looked as if he wanted to cry.

"You did this to me. This is all your fault," Jade screamed at him. "I'll never let you touch me again."

She wouldn't let go of Topaz's hand, so she had to go into the delivery room, too. Jade had to be given additional pain medication before Kobe Ross, a beautiful, healthy boy, entered the world. Nina and Topaz joined Keisha and Eric in the waiting room.

"I never thought I'd hear Jade say the things she said to Sean." Eric laughed.

"She didn't mean it, but if you had that kind of pain, you'd curse, too," Keisha teased. "You cut up when you have a cold."

"Jade had a hard time." A troubled look clouded Nina's pretty face. "When Topaz had Turkey, she just popped out of her."

"Turkey?" Eric was in stitches.

"I told you to stop calling my baby Turkey." Topaz slapped Nina on the thigh with a magazine while Keisha and Eric laughed until they cried. Everyone was tired and they were extremely giddy.

"Okay, but I promise you this." Nina was so serious, everyone stopped laughing and gave her their full attention.

"I am never having a baby. Never . . . that is too much pain for this little body."

Chapter Seventeen

Keisha's heart skipped a beat when she saw him patiently waiting for her. He was sitting at their regular table reading the newspaper.

"We've got to stop meeting this way." She stood behind him and whispered in his ear.

"Not until you find me another restaurant that makes good soul food. I'm not into that Mexican and Thai food everyone eats out here." Germain smiled as the waitress sat a bowl of gumbo in front of him.

"You like Chinese food. Thai is similar, it's just a little sweeter with different spices." She quickly blessed the bowl of gumbo Germain had ordered for her and spread a napkin over her linen pants.

"Maybe I'm just a little homesick. Momma makes a mean pot of gumbo."

He seemed a little distracted. She watched her handsome friend tear into the savory soup and wondered what was really going on inside his head.

"So how come you brought a date to the dinner party? Are you getting serious about her?"

He swallowed the last of the gumbo and looked at Keisha. "I forgot I had already made plans with Sherry, to answer your first question, and no to the second. She wants more, but I don't."

"Why not? She seemed really nice. And you're both doctors. I'm sure you have a lot in common." Keisha wondered why she said that, but she wanted Germain to feel comfortable telling her anything.

"These California sisters are fine, but I want a home girl."

"Like Topaz? She's a home girl." He had finally given her an in to make a pitch for Topaz.

"No, like you."

"Germain, stop."

"I only said that because you were meddling. I know what you're trying to do." He finally laughed.

"I want to see two people that I happen to care about back together. So sue me."

"I know that's what you want, darlin', but that's over." He picked up a piece of golden fried chicken and bit into it.

"Oh, please. You need to stop." Keisha balled up her napkin and threw it at him. "You were so jealous when you saw her with Pete, I thought you were going to beat him down."

"So what's up with that? Is she into white boys now? You said she changed. She sure seemed like the same old Topaz to me with Mr. Blond and Blue Eyes." He tossed the half-eaten drumstick on his plate and pushed it aside.

"Pete is just a friend and the only reason she brought him was that you brought a date. If you noticed, everyone there was with someone and I didn't want her to feel out of place."

"She sure got one fast," he mumbled.

"Look at you, you're jealous now." Keisha pushed aside the rest of her gumbo.

"She did look good. That woman is like a fine bottle of wine that gets better with age."

"Fine as wine and just your kind," Keisha taunted.

He smiled and Keisha wanted to shout. He was finally showing signs of weakening.

"There was a time, but I've moved on." He picked up another piece of chicken and quickly polished it off.

"Moved on? Where, to LA, so you can be near her?"

"Oh, you got jokes. That wasn't about her. This place is great for business." He ate some of the accompanying potato salad.

"Sure it is. So when are you going to admit it?"

He stopped chewing and looked up at Keisha. "Admit what?"

"Admit that you are still in love with Topaz." She had finally said what she had been itching to say for weeks. "The way you brothers live in denial is beyond me."

"Denial?" His voice went up an octave. "I'm not in denial."

"Then why don't you let her see Chris? He needs his mother."

"Because I'm not going to allow her to cause my son any more pain."

She had really pushed a button this time, but she had nothing to lose and everything to gain. "Pain? How do you think Chris feels living in LA and not being able to see his mother? He must be feeling a little rejected."

"I never thought about it that way. He hasn't said anything to me."

"He hasn't?"

"He did at first, but he seems okay with it. Wait . . . he called me crying one day about some article in the paper. A kid said something to him about it at school. See . . . that's the kind of stuff I don't want him exposed to."

"Topaz called me crying about the same article. She's being sued and the press started digging for things to print. Things like that happen to all kids with celebrity parents. It's the price of fame. And no matter what . . . she will always be his mother."

"That's true, but he hasn't been a part of her celebrity. I'm glad she kept our marriage a secret for my son's benefit."

"But you keep forgetting one thing . . . he needs his mother. I know she hurt him. She hurt you and she hurt herself. She keeps beating herself up for it, too. She's changed and there's nothing she wants more than for all of you to be a family again."

"She said that?"

"She says it all the time. She goes to marriage enrichment classes with me. She wants to be a better wife. I probably shouldn't tell you this, but she hasn't even dated since she became single again. She puts all her energy into her daughter and she's a good mother."

"Are you sure we're talking about Topaz, the woman I was married to?"

"Yes." Keisha studied his pensive expression.

"I find that so hard to believe."

"Why? People can change."

"They can, but I can't see her changing."

"Why?" Keisha sipped a glass of water and took a deep breath. She was starting to get frustrated and she needed to relax before she said something she would regret.

"What if I let her back in Chris's life and things are going fine, then all of a sudden she decides she doesn't have time for him?"

"She wouldn't do that."

"How do you know, Keisha? Chris couldn't handle that."

"Are we talking about Chris or are we talking about you?" Keisha spoke softly.

"I came out here and I tried!" he exploded. "I forgave her for never coming home when she promised she would. We had the most wonderful time, the three of us. She was wonderful to Chris. We talked about getting back together. I really thought she had changed then. The next thing I know, she's marrying this Gunther person and my son heard it on the evening news. Did she tell you that?" Germain was almost yelling.

"She told me everything and she regrets every bit of it. Can't you give her another chance?"

Germain sat there holding his head in his hands. After a long silence he finally spoke. "You don't know how badly I would like to do that. I've thought about it and I know there's nothing Chris wants more . . ."

"So do it. Give it a try. Chris has a sister now. Why don't you guys take the girls out to dinner? Turquoise is so pretty. She has those eyes and that blond hair."

"I'm sure she's a little doll." Germain smiled.

"So go for it." Keisha wrote all of Topaz's numbers on a notepad, carefully tore out the page, and handed it to him. He looked at the paper and then at Keisha.

"I'm sorry, Key, but I can't. It took me a long time to get over what she did and I can't take the chance of that happening again. I gotta go." He threw some cash on the table and kissed her on the forehead. "Love you, sweetie."

She watched him drive away and felt like crying. She was so sure her matchmaking would bring them back together. Topaz had made her promise to come by the house and tell her everything as soon as lunch was over. How could she tell her best friend that the man of her dreams wanted nothing to do with her?

Topaz was in the pool with the girls when Keisha drove up. When she saw Keisha's Lexus, the biggest smile spread across her face. She climbed out of the pool, grabbed a towel, stuck her feet in a pair of sandals, and strutted over to meet her.

"Well . . . ?"

"Look at me, Mommy." Kendra dove into the pool and swam toward her.

"Look at me, Auntie Key." Turquoise jumped in and swam after Kendra.

"That was beautiful." Keisha clapped her hands. "You guys are little Esther Williamses. How did Turquoise learn to swim so well?"

"We took lessons together at the Y as soon as she was old enough. They have no fear of the water."

"All right, so what's the scoop on my man, girlfriend? You can't hold out on a sister like that. You know I'm dying to know." She looked at Keisha, who was still trying to find the words to tell her. "What's wrong? He didn't come . . ."

"He came." Her voice was flat and without enthusiasm.

"We're going up to my room so we can talk." She gave Rosa instructions for the children.

"So what happened?" They sat on the bed facing each other.

"He's still hurting, Topaz. He's scared. You really hurt him."

"I know I did, Keisha, but what can I do if he won't let me make it up to him?" The joy had faded from her face.

"It's going to take time, honey. You can't change him, but God can."

"How can God change him? Germain hates me." She was no longer able to hold back the tears.

"No, he doesn't. He just doesn't want to be hurt again. You just hold on to your faith, honey."

"Faith?" Topaz looked at her through teary eyes. "I've had faith since the day he told me he never wanted to see me again. That was two years ago."

"And it may take another two years."

"But that doesn't make sense." Topaz cried from the depths of her soul and Keisha cried with her. She hated seeing her friend in pain and she wanted so badly to help her, but she had done what she could.

"I know it doesn't make sense, but you have to trust God."

"But I don't know how to do that." Topaz wiped her eyes and looked at Keisha, waiting for an answer.

"Did you ever write that letter of apology to Germain?"

"No," she whispered through fresh tears.

"Write it, and then we'll pray."

"Now?" Topaz sniffed.

"Now." Keisha handed her a pen and Topaz produced an unopened box of stationery.

"Nina bought this for me. I've never used it."

She crumpled up several sheets of the elegant paper before she handed Keisha a beautifully written note.

"I forgot how pretty your handwriting is. Do you want me to read this?"

Topaz nodded and Keisha quickly read the brief note that was from her heart and to the point.

"That's nice, T." She took Topaz's hand and prayed that God would heal their relationship. "That's all we can do, now the rest is up to God."

Keisha looked at her watch as she pulled into the driveway. She and Eric had dinner plans and she was running late. In her class, they had discussed the importance of keeping a marriage alive, so now Eric and she had a date night once a week, when they went out and did something together, as a couple.

She rushed into the house and was surprised to find Sean, talking to her husband. They seemed to be having a serious conversation, probably about basketball.

She kissed Eric and dashed upstairs to change. It was strange to see Sean at the house. Even though they only lived minutes away from his place in the Marina, he rarely, if ever, came by in the evening. Eric usually had a game or he was out of town. Sean met him every morning him to work out.

She jumped into the shower and felt her body relax the moment the warm water pelted her skin, but she couldn't help thinking about Sean. There was something strange about his visit, but what was even stranger was the forlorn look on his handsome face.

Chapter Eighteen

Jade walked through the gallery admiring its jade and gold marble interior as if she were seeing it for the very first time. Akiba and Kiyoko had kept things running smoothly while she was out having the baby.

She looked down at the tiny sleeping baby wearing a little mint green cap and jumper, wrapped up in a blanket, and gently kissed him on the forehead.

"My little man."

She carried him into the back workroom where Kiyoko did matting and she painted. Her workspace had been tidied, but the painting she had been working on when she went into labor was sitting on the easel.

"Look, Kobe, that's the painting your mother was working on the day you were born. You really demanded some attention that day, but you are your father's son."

She placed the diaper bag on the floor and carefully lifted the infant out of the carrier and placed him in the crib. She had purchased three different cribs when she shopped for baby furniture.

She prepared a palette of watercolors and sat down in front of the painting. "I've carried you around inside for so long, it feels weird for you to be over there sleeping."

She put the paints down and felt her stomach. Jade had picked up an extra fifteen pounds. She carried it well on her five-foot-nine-inch frame, but she was still uncomfortable with the changes in her body.

Uninspired, she stared at the canvas for several minutes before getting a fresh one. She put on a CD of classical music and pulled her stool and easel next to Kobe's crib. She took a charcoal and began sketching the soft curves of her son's face. Moments later, she dabbed a brush into a glob of reddish brown paint.

"I cannot believe you are back in the studio with this baby. Is it okay for him to be around all this paint?" Nina kneeled on the floor beside the baby's crib.

"You scared me." Jade put down her brush and pushed herself back from the easel. "I didn't hear you come in."

"That's because you were in a world of your own." Nina lifted the infant out of the crib and cuddled him to her breast. "You are too beautiful, Kobe Ross. She sat in a chair and softly stroked the infant across his back. "He is too precious."

"I know," Jade agreed. "Watch out, you're looking a little too comfortable there. You'll be a mother yet." Jade smiled as Nina continued to make a fuss over her son.

"You know my thoughts on that subject. Between this little angel and my Turkey, I have enough babies. But seriously, is it okay for him to be around this paint?"

"You sound like my husband. Have you been talking to him? Do you think I would do something that could harm my own baby?" She sat down and returned to her painting.

"No, I don't think you would do something to hurt Kobe. I was only asking because I was concerned." She watched Jade dip her brush into a dab of mint and quickly duplicated the little cap her son was wearing. "Hey, that looks just like him. You are so talented. Why don't you do more portraits?"

"I made more money from the scenery." She moved to another section and soon she could see his jumper. "Watercolors don't have fumes and they aren't harmful. I double-checked with his pediatrician to be sure."

Nina placed the baby back in the crib and sat down next to her friend. Something was obviously bothering her. "Is something wrong, Jade?"

"No." She was working on his black hair.

"This is me. What's up?" She watched her paint Kobe's long eyelashes. "Are you still going out of town?"

"Yes, for a week." She sat back and studied her work.

"How does Sean feel about this?"

Jade ran her hands through her hair, which was already back down to her shoulders. "He hates it. He thought I was going to stay home once Kobe was born. He is so old-fashioned. He wants me to be a boring housewife like his mother, Karla, and Keisha. I am nobody's housewife. I've got people to see, places to go."

"Did you guys talk about this before you were married?" Nina watched her make finishing touches on the painting.

"Yes, but he knew I had a career. I was working when he met me."

"Were you this busy?"

"No, that all happened after I became Mrs. Jade Ross." She got up and rinsed out her brushes. "I'll try and cut back, but I didn't expect to become pregnant the same month I was married. And Sean needs a lot of attention. And now I have him. I'm not superwoman. I'm looking forward to going away so I can get a full night of sleep."

Kobe woke up yelling.

"I'll feed him." Nina found a bottle in Jade's diaper bag, heated it in the microwave, and sprinkled a few drops of formula on the back of her hand before she stuck the nipple in his mouth. He sucked on the bottle and held on to Nina's finger.

"He is so sweet." Nina looked up at Jade, who was standing over her, and smiled. "I don't see how you could leave him."

"It'll be hard." Jade brushed a lock of his hair. "But he'll be fine with his nanny and his daddy."

"Does he look like Sean or what? He spit him out. Those Rosses sure have some strong genes." Nina sat the baby up so she could burp him. When he let out a big belch, both of the women laughed.

"You go, Kobe." Jade smiled and her almond eyes became two slits.

"He has your eyes. There's no mistake about that."

"Those are his grandfather's Japanese eyes. When the girls look into them, they'll be lost forever."

"Oh, no, another heartbreaker. And he's fine, too. Don't hurt 'em too bad, Kobe." Nina placed the baby back inside the carrier and Jade set the picture of her son aside to dry.

"We're having him dedicated when I get back from Washington, and I want you to be his godmother. Sean chose Keisha and Eric as godparents and his brother Kirk. His father is going to do the ceremony at the ranch." She added some additional color to the unfinished island scenery.

"Kirk has a twin, right?" Nina walked around the room mindlessly looking at paintings and art equipment.

"Kyle's the other one. He's coming."

"He's single, right?"

"Yes."

"Good, so you can hook a sister up. He's fine."

"What?" Jade stopped painting and turned around to look at her. "You're serious, aren't you?"

"Yes. Kirk is one fine man and if he's a twin . . . He gives me a fever."

Jade screamed with laughter and covered her mouth. She had forgotten about the baby. "Just think, if I hooked you guys up, you'd be my sister-in-law."

"There you go. I asked to meet the brother and you've already got us married. I told you I'm not ready for that."

"You sure aren't. What about Jamil?"

"What about him?"

"Ooh." Jade picked up her brush. "I'm not getting in the middle of this. What did you do with that ring?"

"I'm going to give it back. I can't marry Jamil. You made me realize that."

"Me?" Jade came and stood next to her friend.

"You told me the reason you married Sean was that you couldn't live without him. I can live without Jamil."

"No one should get married if they're not in love. It's hard enough when you are in love."

Sean was at home reading a book when Jade arrived with Kobe. She set the baby in his carrier on the floor and plopped down beside Sean. "Hi, honey, how are you?"

"Missing my family." He snapped the book closed and took the baby out of the carrier and began to fuss over him.

"Hey, can his mother get a little love, too?" Jade was almost pouting.

"I'm sorry." He kissed her on the cheek and cuddled her with one arm while he held Kobe in the other until he opened his eyes and cried.

"Okay, sweetheart, Daddy's right here." Jade smiled when he jumped up and got the diaper bag. He talked to Kobe the entire time while he changed him and heated up his formula.

"I'm going to take a quick shower," she said. "If he's asleep, why don't you join me?"

She winked before she left the room. After her conversation with Nina about marriage, she had decided to plan a quiet romantic evening. It had been a long time since there was any activity in the bedroom and they were long overdue.

Her doctor had given has the go-ahead, and even though she was feeling self-conscious about the changes in her body, she felt it was time to heat things back up again. She had refused his advances several times because she felt too fat and she had been too embarrassed to tell him.

She had called in for an order of their favorite Chinese food for them to eat by candlelight. She was undressing when Sean walked into the bedroom.

"Honey, Kobe is asleep. I have to make a run to the airport to pick up my mother. Can you make that shower quick?" He looked at his watch and looked at her.

"Your mother? She's coming, here? Tonight?" Jade sat on the bed and looked up at him.

"Yes."

"Why? The christening isn't until next week."

"I know, but she decided to come early when I told her you were going to be out of town for a week, so she could spend some time with us. She didn't want us to be alone."

"And when were you planning to tell me this? When she walked in the door?"

"I didn't think you'd mind since you're not going to be here."

"Did it ever occur to you that I could have made plans for us tonight?"

"Plans . . . since when do you make plans for us? You're always too tired to do anything. So no, I didn't think to tell you my mother was coming. You're too busy trying to get away from me and the baby."

"Sean, that is not true and you know it. And Kobe has a nanny, so this is just an excuse for you to be up under your mother, like a baby. That's what this really is. You are such a mama's boy. You need to grow up."

She wanted to kill him. She went into the bathroom and slammed the door. Moments later, she heard the front door slam.

Another fight.

She felt the hot tears on her face even beneath the water of the steam shower.

She was wearing pajamas and eating Chinese food when Sean arrived with his mother. She took her plate and went into the bedroom to watch television. She could hear them making a fuss over Kobe, and then she heard his mother tell him to go spend time with his wife. She cut off the lights and pretended to be asleep.

"Jade, honey."

She felt him sit on the edge of the bed and drop his Nikes on the floor one at a time. She knew without looking that he was stuffing his socks in his shoes. She waited for the sound his nylon sweats made when he pulled those off and then she felt his full weight on the bed as he rolled over next to her. She felt him cuddle up behind her and his arms wrap around her. His body felt so good next to hers. That was her cue to turn over and face him and let nature take its course.

"Leave me alone, Sean." Jade surprised even herself by the harsh tone in her voice. "Go sleep with your mother."

They said very little to each other the next morning. She called Nina from the limo and told her everything.

"I can understand him letting his mother come. She wanted to see her new grandson and you are on your way out of town. You need to apologize. You were wrong."

"But I didn't feel comfortable with his mother in the next room." She knew she had messed up, and Nina wasn't helping her feel any less guilty.

"Did you tell him that?"

"No."

"You were wrong, girlfriend." Nina bit into a slice of toast and looked at Topaz, who was pouring a cup of coffee.

"We can all take a lesson from my cousin. Don't be like her. If she could do it over, she would in a heartbeat. You have to keep a balance. Men want attention. They want to be pampered. They want to feel special and know they come first and that you don't ever take them for granted."

"And what do I get for all that?" Jade was being difficult and she knew it. "Nothing but a spoiled brat and hard way to go."

Chapter Nineteen

Topaz flipped through the pages of the document and quickly signed her name by all the indications and pushed the document back across the desk to her attorney. She had taken Keisha's advice and agreed to an out-of-court settlement with Gunther's family for more than three million dollars.

The Lawrences would receive two million dollars to divide and spend as they pleased, one million to be held in trust for Gunther Jr., by Rosalyn, and another half a million to Carmen Martinez. The agreement also stipulated that there would be no further lawsuits or payments made to anyone, or contact with her daughter.

With that out of the way, she drove into the posh day spa in Encino, where she met Keisha for a day of pampering. They started with a honey-almond and papaya facial, a deep tissue massage, followed by a sea-salt body scrub. She sipped a hot cup of herbal tea while her feet soaked in a foot spa.

"Damn, I wish I had something stronger." She set the cup down in its saucer and pushed it away. "I wonder if they serve champagne here."

"All right, girlfriend, no champagne. You will not drink anymore to cover your pain."

"Who's in pain?" Topaz looked around for the waitress that had served the tea. "I'm celebrating. The lawsuit with the Lawrence family is over. No more court and no more press."

The waitress came and offered Topaz a smoothie. The establishment didn't serve wine or spirits.

"You heifer. You knew that when you chose this place." Topaz made the funniest face and Keisha laughed until she cried. "I'll choose the spa next time and I'll make sure they serve wine and spirits."

A waitress brought Keisha a veggie burger on a whole-wheat bun with sprouts, Monterey Jack cheese, and homemade mayo. She also had a fruit salad and an apple spritzer.

"That looks good. Can I have a bite?" Topaz sniffed her food hungrily.

"You're as bad as Kendra." She cut the sandwich in half and offered it to Topaz, who took a bite and ordered the same thing as Keisha.

"Are you going to allow Turquoise to spend time with Rosalyn again now that everything is over?" Keisha watched the woman dry her foot and file her toenails.

"No and I don't want to talk about that now." She handed her manicurist a bottle of nail polish and watched her paint her fingernails a cool shade of green. "So who are the Lakers playing tonight?"

"San Antonio Spurs. It should be a good game. I can't believe you're finally coming to a game now that the season is over."

"I'm sorry, Key. I've been in the studio a lot so I thought I should spend the time with Turquoise. We watch Uncle Eric on TV. And I want to meet this fine-ass Robert Horry that Nina's kicking my boy Jamil to the curb for."

"She broke up with Jamil?" The manicurist was working on Keisha's other foot now.

"Not yet. I think she's crazy. That man loves her. You should see the ring he gave her that she never wore."

"He gave her a ring?"

"Yes, a serious rock that she keeps locked it in a box with her weed. She thinks I don't know. She is so funny."

"Nina gets high?"

"Her one vice. She swears it's an aphrodisiac. She used to do coke, too. She had me doing it. We were social users, as they say. We both stopped after Gunther died, but she still smokes her weed."

"She doesn't look the type." Keisha was astonished.

"I don't know what the type is, but that's Nina. Wild child. When I first came to LA, she used to tell me I was a square."

"You a square? Now that's funny." Keisha laughed.

Topaz's two-way beeped and she opened it. "Yes, I'm still going to the game tonight." She spoke as she typed. "I'm leaving my car at the house and she's even driving so we won't be late. We'll meet you there." Topaz snapped her new toy closed and smiled at Keisha. "She must have heard us talking about her."

They arrived at the game in plenty of time before the tip-off, so they sat in the stands and people-watched.

"Look at all the hoochies." Topaz's eyes followed a woman with a tight, short dress. "If she bends over she'll show everything she's got."

"I think that was the point." Keisha pointed out a woman sitting below her with a friend. "That one had designs on Eric."

Topaz looked the woman up and down. "Please. She's no competition for you. None of these women are. I hope these heifers weren't the reason you started wearing makeup."

"It seems kind of silly now, but I was feeling a little insecure when we first moved here. But you really helped me. The move did, too."

"Really? You're kidding." Topaz was shocked. "What did I do?"

Nina arrived wearing her black and gold snakeskin pants, looking like a million dollars.

"Look at you." Keisha grinned. "You look so cute. I wish I had the nerve to wear those pants. They're hot."

"Only Nina could wear those." Topaz laughed. "Beauty is wasted on the young. Do you see that body? Those boobs will be perky forever."

Nina ignored them and tossed her hair and they saw her shirt was backless.

"Work it, girlfriend." Keisha laughed and turned to Topaz. "You're one to talk about perky. And no one would ever think that body had two babies."

"I had these girls lifted. Everybody does it." Topaz looked at the sleeveless green fitted sweater she had chosen to wear with her black leather pants. "A girl's gotta do what a girl's gotta do."

The three of them were cackling like hens when a soft masculine voice interrupted.

"Hello, ladies. I feel like I'm interrupting the party, but I'm sitting here, too." Sean gave them a Pepsodent smile and sat down beside Nina. He was wearing a nice pair of slacks with a jade shirt.

"My God, that man is too fine," Nina whispered through gritted teeth to Topaz.

"Hey, sweetie. I didn't know you were coming tonight." Keisha leaned across Topaz and Nina and smiled at Sean.

"Jade's out of town and my mom is with Kobe so I thought I'd come see my boy do his thing tonight." His smile was warm and genuine.

"Welcome to the party." Nina smiled.

"Speaking of parties, I expect to see all of you at the ranch next weekend for Kobe's dedication. We didn't do invitations because it's just family, and all of you are family."

"Do you ever regret letting that go?" Nina whispered to Topaz once the game started.

"No. You know that," Topaz whispered back. "Don't start bothering me about Sean because you've got the hots. Remember he's your best friend's husband."

"I'd swear your elevator doesn't go all the way to the top floor."
Nina pinched her on the thigh.

Sean waited with the ladies after the game for Eric and Robert
Horry. There was finally a consensus for dinner in Beverly Hills,
where Sean was overwhelmed with memories of basketball. It was
the first time he had been out to dinner with Eric after a game since
he had moved to Los Angeles.

Nina excused herself and whispered in Topaz's ear that she was
going salsa dancing.

"I'm telling Jamil, you bad girl." She grinned at Nina as she left.

"I remember a night in New York, similar to this, when we first
met these gorgeous ladies." Eric smiled at Sean and then at his
wife.

"Topaz, did I ever thank you for introducing me to my beautiful
wife and the woman of my dreams?" Eric smiled at Keisha and
kissed her gently on the lips while Topaz and Sean smiled. Even a
blind man could have seen the love that resonated between them.

"It was my pleasure, Eric."

Topaz's last words were muffled because a thick lump had suddenly formed in her throat. She fumbled in her purse for her compact and quickly brushed a tear away. She was happy for Keisha and
she knew how she felt. She had had the love of a wonderful man
and traded it in for a singing career. Germain had even given her a
second chance. There was no one to blame except herself.

She looked at Sean, who was smiling at Keisha and Eric, and realized she had better make a quick exit before she started crying all
over the place. She had no car because she had ridden with Keisha.
Sean had dropped Eric off before the game and she had felt like a
third wheel riding with them to the restaurant.

"People, it's been real, but I'm calling it a night." She picked up
her bag and took some cash out of her wallet.

"Don't insult me by trying to pay for dinner. It's because of you and Sean that we're here tonight." He was making goo-goo eyes at Keisha again. They were so sweet it was sickening.

"She's not going anywhere, because I have to take her home." Keisha looked away from Eric to look at Topaz.

"You're not taking me anywhere. You're going to sit right here and keep making goo-goo eyes with your husband. I live ten minutes away. I can take a taxi." She kissed them both and said goodbye before they could say another word.

"I can take you home." She was surprised to find Sean standing behind her.

"Thanks, Sean, but no. I only live a few minutes away. I can take a taxi. You go back with Eric and Keisha."

"You want me to go back in there with them? Not that they'd even notice I was there, but I would really feel like a third party."

"I know, huh?" Topaz laughed. "I felt the same way."

Sean drove through the gate onto the Bel Air property.

"This is really nice." The sprawling grounds were brightly lit and expertly manicured. Water cascaded down the wall of the pool and gurgled over rocks.

"Thanks. It seems a little big sometimes, but it's home. Would you like to come in?"

Topaz didn't know why she asked and she was equally surprised when he said yes. She led him through the house and into the playroom. Sean looked around at the restored Wurlitzer jukebox, the popcorn machine, and old-fashioned soda fountain, and grinned.

"This is tight." He went over to the jukebox and studied the selections.

"I'll be right back. Make yourself at home. There's quarters for the jukebox in the ashtray or you can turn on the TV."

She went into the kitchen for a bottle of Cristal and champagne glasses. When she returned a Marvin Gaye CD was playing.

"How about we toast your beautiful son?" She poured the

sparkling liquid into the flutes and handed him one. "To four more sons so you can have your own basketball team."

He grinned and they clicked glasses. "Those were my intentions when I named my son Kobe, but I don't think so. My wife said one is all I get."

"She might change her mind. She's still recovering." Topaz smiled.

"Jade told me how you were there for her. She was really frightened. Thank you so much."

"I remember what it was like when I had Chris. I was afraid, too. My ex-husband is a doctor so he was a big help."

She poured herself another glass of champagne. She had wanted a glass for weeks, but ever since Keisha showed her how she had been using it to mask her pain, she had stopped drinking it. She was enjoying the conversation with Sean. They always seemed to disagree when they had tried to date, but now she felt quite comfortable with her old friend. Married life had really mellowed him.

"So how are things with you?" Topaz pulled one leg under her.

"Pretty good. I've really been thinking about returning to basketball. I could be a Laker with Eric."

"You miss it, don't you?"

"Yeah, I do. I thought my sports management business would keep me occupied. But it's not the same. I have a lot of meetings. Being there tonight and going out afterward really brought back a lot of memories."

"How does Jade feel about you getting back into sports? You'll be on the road a lot away from your family."

"She wants me to play. She's busy a lot and she thinks I need something to do." He poured himself another glass of champagne.

"What about the baby?"

"She's already hired a nanny. Kobe's at home with my mother. Jade's in DC for a week."

"That's hard . . . dual careers, but someone has to be willing to give in for things to work. I learned that the hard way." She poured the last of the champagne into her glass.

"But she doesn't have to work. She can stay home with the baby."

"But she loves her work. Have you ever thought about taking Kobe and his nanny and traveling with her? You guys could have fun."

"I never thought about that. I always thought my wife would stay home and I would work. That's how my parents did it."

"But things are different now. There are a lot of us women who work because we enjoy it. Why do men think a woman doesn't need him if she's able to take care of herself?"

"But God created us to be providers." He was really sincere.

"That's true, but times have changed. It's not like you have to go out and hunt for food all day." Topaz laughed. "There are plenty of other things a man can provide for a woman and they're not just tangible." She was amazed at how much she had retained from the marriage classes. "For instance . . . I don't need a man to provide for me, but does that mean I don't need a man?"

"No." She could tell Sean was really thinking. "So what do you need?"

"New-millennium women need our men to love us and cherish us. We need you to be our friends and listen to us. And when we tell you our problems it's not for you to solve them. We just need you to listen."

"You make a lot of sense. . . . Jade's always telling me I'm old-fashioned, but she never told me why."

"See all those ways I just told you how a woman needs a man? And that wasn't everything."

"Yeah, I know. Can you write them down? I need to try and remember this." They both laughed and Sean put some more coins into the jukebox.

"So how are things with you and Germain?"

"He doesn't want me." She looked down into her empty glass and then at him.

"He's a fool."

"It's all my fault." She had to whisper because she had suddenly

121

lost her voice. She felt the tears that she had tried to fight back earlier well up in her eyes and this time the tears won.

Sean pulled her into his arms as she cried. Her entire body caved in next to his strength. It had been years since she was held in a man's arms and she felt herself melting. With very little effort her lips found his. They were positively delightful. To her surprise he kissed her back with intense passion.

Neither one of them was thinking as she led him upstairs to her bedroom. She undressed him and then herself and climbed into bed beside him. She was mindless as she felt her body respond to his gentle touch. It had been too long.

Hours later, waves of guilt flooded her mind. She couldn't even look at him as she walked him downstairs to the door. What had started out as a beautiful evening between two old friends had ended in disaster. She wished she had never invited him in, but there was no way to undo the terrible wrong she had done.

How can I ever face Jade or Sean again?

A ringing phone wakened her from a restless sleep. It was morning. She listened to it ring several more times before she snatched it up. Whatever and whoever it was had to be faced.

She couldn't believe it when she heard the voice she had longed for, the one with an ever so slight, but definite southern twang. The voice she never thought she would hear again, and on her telephone.

"I got your letter, Topaz. We need to talk."

Was that really Germain?

She pinched herself to see if she was dreaming and hoped the previous evening had all been a nightmare and she was just waking up.

Chapter Twenty

Nina sifted through her lingerie drawer searching for the perfect lingerie to wear under the crisp white Armani pantsuit hanging on the closet door. Everything had to be absolutely perfect today. She picked up the phone, started to make a call, hung it back up, and trotted out of the room and down the hall past Turquoise's room into her cousin's.

"I cannot believe you are still in bed." She pulled open the heavy mauve drapes and light flooded the bedroom. "Kobe's dedication is this afternoon and we have to drive all the way to Santa Barbara."

Topaz rolled over and pulled the covers over her head. "Leave me alone. I'm not going."

Nina pulled the covers back and off the bed onto the floor. "Girl, cut the drama and get up. I can't be late. I'm Kobe's godmother."

Topaz sat up in bed and looked at Nina. "I'm not feeling well. You'd better go without me." She pulled the covers back on the bed and got underneath them. "I won't be missed. It's not like I'm Jade's best friend. She doesn't even like me." She buried her face halfway behind a pillow and looked up at Nina through one eye.

"She does so like you. She told me to be sure you came. You've been her hero ever since you helped her when the baby was born."

"She was drugged," Topaz mumbled and placed a hand on her forehead. "I think I'm coming down with the flu or something." She coughed and blew her nose in a tissue to prove her point. "I'm not in any condition to be around a newborn little baby. There's a gift for them on the dining room table."

"Whatever. I've got to go." Nina stared at the lump in the bed and wondered why Topaz really didn't want to go out to the ranch to a party with her friends. Something's up, she reasoned, and left the room.

She had never been to Sean's ranch in Santa Barbara. She had planned to go up with Jade for a weekend, but they never made it.

My, God, this place is beautiful. She had noticed that all of the estates faced the ocean as she followed the directions Sean had given her. Endless miles of placid blue water coupled with a serenity that was heavenly. She was in another world.

It even smells different out here. I am having a talk with Miss Thing. She has got to start spending more time up here with her husband.

Green and silver balloons adorned the black wrought-iron gate. Nina pulled up next to the squawk box, but before she could push a button the gate rolled open and she pulled into the circular mosaic drive next to Jade's convertible two-seater Beemer.

She carefully stepped out of the truck and put on the jacket to her suit. She reached for the packages and her purse and when she turned around a gorgeous chocolate brother with close-cut hair and twinkling eyes was standing in front of her. Just the sight of him took her breath away because he was fine, dangerously fine.

"I'll take these." He took the presents while Nina tried to think of something to say. "I'm Kobe's uncle, Kyle." He smiled Sean's same Pepsodent smile. "And you must be Nina."

She liked the way he said her name. No one had ever said it quite that way. She knew immediately that he was spoiled and used to having his way with women. *He thinks he's cute.*

At some point her feisty spirit returned and she was able to breathe again. She took off her sunglasses and looked directly into his eyes. "Who told you I was Nina?"

He adjusted his tie just below his Adam's apple and licked his lips. "Because a woman as fine as you has to be called Nina."

She tried not to smile as he led her into the house. He was good. *No wonder he isn't married.* She knew he had more women than he knew what to do with . . . and he would never add her to that list. *Not in this lifetime.*

"Whatever he said, don't blame me." Sean greeted her with an identical smile. The Ross brothers were too much . . . too charming, too fine, and too good to be true.

"Where's Jade?" She needed a distraction from fine chocolate men.

"She's upstairs getting the baby ready. You can go up, but I want you to meet my parents first."

Sean took her into the living room and introduced her to his and Jade's parents. By the time she had greeted Eric, Keisha, Kirk, and Karla, Jade was downstairs. She looked more beautiful than Nina had ever seen her. She had dropped the weight from the baby and her shoulder-length hair was tapered and silky straight. She looked like a Japanese Barbie with dark skin.

"Girlfriend, you are stunning." Nina kissed her on the cheek and took the baby.

"I am?" She adjusted the white cap on Kobe's black hair and looked at Nina.

"Yes, you are. Don't you know that?"

Jade shrugged and looked down at the floor.

"And so are you, handsome," Nina said. She kissed Kobe on the cheek and looked at Jade, who was watching Sean talk with his brothers.

"I want you to meet my parents." Jade quickly brushed away a tear, grabbed Nina by the hand, and led her across the room.

"Sean already introduced me." Nina really wanted to find out why Jade was tripping, but feared if she pushed the subject any further, Jade would be in tears.

Between her and Topaz, I'll be doing more drugs than I already do.

"Father, this is my best friend, Miss Nina Beaubien. She's really like a sister."

Paul Kimura was tall and very handsome. Jade favored him a lot. "So this is the young lady I've heard so much about. It's a pleasure, Miss Beaubien." He bowed and kissed Nina's hand. Jade laughed and kissed her father. "He is such a flirt."

"This is my mother, Judith." Jade had inherited her flawless skin, lithe dancer's body, and full luscious lips. "Doesn't Nina look like a dancer, Mother? She's works for *MTV* and she's going to publish a novel."

"That's fabulous, Nina. And you certainly keep yourself fit. Perhaps you can assist my daughter with her exercise regimen so she can lose the last of that fat from the baby."

"Mother, I've been trying." Jade looked down at her stomach and frowned. "Nina and I already have plans to exercise together and I'm getting a navel ring."

"A navel ring. That's interesting. You ladies might want to take some belly dancing classes. When I had Jade, I was up and dancing the following week. I couldn't lose my position with the dance theater."

"Belly dancing. Isn't Mother funny?" Jade laughed as the ladies excused themselves.

"She's a riot."

No wonder the girl doesn't think she's beautiful. Mom is loony tunes. She couldn't understand a mother criticizing her own daughter. She glanced at Mr. Kimura. *And he's probably henpecked.*

"Did you meet Kyle?" Jade looked across the room at him and back at Nina. "I told him to be nice to you."

"I met him."

"Isn't he fine?" Jade nudged her and grinned.

"Yeah, and he knows it."

"True, but you can handle that. You're just the thing to rock his world. He's a senior vice president for American Express in international finance. He's very smart. He travels often. He's got investments, stocks . . . the man is a zillionaire. All of them are, because Kyle is the one who tells them what to do with their money."

They both looked at Kyle, who was talking with Eric and Keisha. It was obvious that he was telling them something very interesting.

"Sean will be thirty-one so the twins are thirty-two because they're a year apart. He's never had a serious girlfriend and his father wants him settle down and get married. All of the Ross boys do what Mommy and Daddy tell them."

"Girl, stop. And why are you tell me all this?" Nina smirked.

"Information. Knowledge is power, girlfriend." Jade made one of her silly faces and Nina finally laughed.

"You should have been on stage. You missed your calling."

They were still laughing when Sean walked up and took the baby from Nina. "Excuse me, ladies, but this little man is needed for photos." He carried the baby to his mother and Jade sucked her teeth.

"Mama's boy."

"What is up with the two of you?" Nina definitely sensed a chill in the air.

"Nothing. Not a thing." She spoke with a Jamaican accent, something Nina never heard her do.

"Something is going on."

"Nothing's going on. That's the problem. Things have just been a bit chilly since we had that fight before I went to DC. His family is here now and he's in his zone. I usually just chill when they come around. . . . Hey, where's Topaz? I thought she was coming. If it hadn't been for Topaz and you, Kobe might not be here since his father was a knucklehead and left his cell phone in his bag. I swear if I didn't love that man, I would kill him."

"That's good to know."

She watched Sean taking photographs with his brothers and Eric and wondered why he wasn't taking pictures with his wife. She had done all the work and he was taking all the bows. *Men.*

"Topaz wasn't feeling well. She felt like she was coming down with the flu and didn't think it was a good idea for her to be around the baby." Nina knew it was a crock, but she was used to making excuses for Topaz when she didn't want to make an appearance at some event. The possibility of her infecting the baby was reasonable and considerate, something Jade and Sean and anyone else that asked for her would believe, but Nina wasn't buying it for one minute.

"She sent a gift."

"That was sweet of Topaz. I'll call her to be sure she's okay."

Sean interrupted their conversation to tell them it was time for the dedication to begin. He took them both by the hand and escorted them out back to a white gazebo with the ocean for a backdrop. There were more green and silver balloons and Jade's painting of Kobe was framed and hung.

A podium was set up with a microphone. The Ross family and friends were seated as Kenneth Ross, equally as handsome and as fit as one of his sons, stood behind it and opened with a prayer. He spoke briefly about children being a gift from God and how the parents were responsible for teaching their children the ways of God and guiding them into purpose. Kyle, who had slid in next to Nina, leaned over and whispered in her ear.

"I've got a bottle of champagne I'd like to pour all over your body and taste you."

Nina's body grew hot and she shivered at the same time. She could still feel the print of his warm breath in her ear. *How dare he say something like that to me?* She was angry because his words had affected her. She looked at him as he sat there, focused on his father, the epitome of innocence.

"Nina." Jade was calling her. Everyone was standing and they were waiting for her. She was so embarrassed. Somehow she collected her thoughts and listened to Pastor Ross talk about the responsibilities of the godparents. They had the same duties as the parents.

Nina decided she had better buy herself a Bible and read it—she was going to be a good godmother to Kobe. She hadn't been inside a church for years except to attend someone's wedding.

Pastor Ross prayed for his grandson and held Kobe up to heaven. Kobe seemed as if he knew what was going on. He straightened the lace gown and handed him back to Sean. It was over. Kobe sighed and snuggled up in his father's arms and went to sleep.

"Where were you when Papa Ross called your name?" Jade placed Kobe in his crib and took Nina on a tour of the second floor of the house.

"You don't even want to know."

When she returned downstairs, Kyle appeared and handed her a plate of food. They had hired a caterer who had prepared a wonderful Cajun buffet.

"The pasta is really good."

Nina took the plate and looked at him. She had never met a man so full of confidence. *He is six years older, could that be the difference?*

"Thank you." She sat down and they chatted for hours. She had never talked that long with Jamil about anything. He would talk about his artists and music for a quick minute and then he just wanted sex.

"You're not a heathen, are you?" Kyle gave her a smile that had her melting. "You can't be the mother of my children if you are."

Nina opened up her mouth to protest and closed it. For once, she had nothing to say.

Chapter Twenty-one

Keisha eagerly searched the faces of the passengers who had just begun to enter the terminal from the Delta flight from Atlanta. She could barely stand still as she watched her handsome father approach her. His salt-and-pepper hair reeked of sophistication and intelligence.

"Daddy, Daddy. Here we are." She squeezed Kendra's hand and tried to remember she was a mother now because she had always been a "Daddy's girl."

"Hi, baby girl." Dr. Nichols grabbed Keisha with one arm and swooped up Kendra with the other. "How are my sweet girls?"

He kissed them both and the three of them walked through the airport holding hands. They collected his luggage and led the sky-cap out to a stretch limousine.

"A limo?" He looked at Keisha. "I feel special."

"Daddy, you are very special."

"Look at you two, so glamorous and sophisticated. California agrees with you, Keisha."

"I love it here, Daddy. I didn't think I would, but I do."

"Good, baby. I don't want my little girl unhappy."

"Little girl? Daddy, I am a married woman with a daughter."

"And a very pretty one, too." He pulled Kendra's ponytail. "But you'll always be my little girl."

She smiled and cuddled under her father's arm, content to be his girl again.

"Eric loves it, too. He said this season has been the best one of his career."

"Really? That's fantastic. I always see him in the sports highlights. Does he have a game tonight?"

"Yes, in Phoenix. He'll be back tomorrow. You know we're in the playoffs now." She rarely boasted about Eric's accomplishments to anyone, but her father was an avid basketball fan and loved to hear any news about Eric. Sometimes she wished Eric had taken a position with the Hawks so she could be near her family and her father could attend the games. They had talked about purchasing a home in Atlanta but that was before the move to Los Angeles. Eric was talking about building a home in Westlake Village and Keisha liked the idea.

"I know how busy you're going to be while you're here, Daddy, so I hired a limo so I don't have to drive and we can relax and talk."

"That was a good idea. I have lots of meetings but I want to spend as much time as I can with all of you."

He looked out at the traffic on the freeway. They were going to the marina for a late lunch and then on to the Children's Hospital in Hollywood.

"Have you found a cure for the sickle cell disease yet?" She cut Kendra's burger in half and put some catsup on her french fries.

"No, baby. It's unfortunate. If we had the kind of dollars available for research that have been put into some of the other diseases, I'm sure we'd have a cure by now."

Keisha cut her steak and chewed thoughtfully. "Do you think people don't care because this basically only affects African-Americans?"

"I would love to think that was true, but the reality of the situation is that African-Americans are unconcerned. They are pretty much uninformed unless someone in their immediate family has it, and then they're embarrassed to talk about it."

"Why is that?"

"Ignorance mainly, which is a result of a lack of education about the disease. Teenagers are especially at risk of having a child with the disease if they are a carrier of the trait and they're having unprotected sex. But enough about that, I want to hear all about you guys."

They talked about Kendra's school and friends: Topaz and Germain, Chris, whom Keisha still hadn't seen, Sean and Jade, and Nina. As Keisha was talking about them, she suddenly realized how much they had all become an integral part of her life. They were her family now, and during the short time she had lived in California, their lives were very intertwined. Jade still kept a friendly but marked distance, but Keisha was praying about that, and she was Kobe's godmother, so she would always be a part of his life. Friendship was a matter of time.

After Kendra left for school the following morning, the limo arrived to take Keisha and Dr. Nichols to the Children's Hospital. There was a special research grant that had been recently obtained that would be shared among several hospitals. Keisha sat in on a budget meeting and listened to how the money would be divided. What had seemed like a large sum of money was nothing and there was so much that still couldn't be done.

She was still thinking about the lack of funding when they visited some of the children who were patients. Keisha was so absorbed in her thoughts that she didn't recognize the young woman standing in front of her listening to a little boy's lungs. She scribbled some notes on a chart and walked over to her.

"Keisha Johnson, right?" She smiled and extended a hand.

She had on green scrubs and a stethoscope hung around her neck. Keisha knew she had met her somewhere but she couldn't remember where.

"I'm Rosalyn Lawrence, Topaz's sister-in-law, Turquoise's aunt . . ."

"Rosalyn, yes." Keisha gave her a hug. "I didn't know you were a doctor."

"This is the first year of my residence in pediatric hematology. You never looked at my card." Her smile was still warm.

"I'm sorry, but things have been so crazy ever since that day. You're right. I'm here with my father, Dr. Melvyn Nichols, from Atlanta."

"Dr. Nichols is your father?" She was in awe. "My goodness, woman. You're surrounded by famous men."

Keisha laughed and introduced the two. Dr. Nichols was very familiar with Rosalyn's research skills and wanted to lure her to Atlanta to head up his research team.

"Is he serious?" Rosalyn asked Keisha.

"He never says anything he doesn't mean."

"That's definitely an offer worth considering. I'm torn. I love working with the children." She watched Dr. Nichols chat with a little girl who had been complaining of pain. "Speaking of children, have you made any progress with my sister-in-law?"

Topaz would lose it if she ever heard you refer to her as her sister-in-law.

"No, I haven't. But I promise to think of something soon. I still have your card in my wallet and I'll give you a call as soon as I do."

She rushed to join her father. They were having a big dinner meeting with more doctors later that night and she wanted to spend time with Kendra before she left.

"Daddy, I've been thinking. I want to help you raise money for research. I could get Topaz to put on a benefit concert. We could have it at Sean and Jade's ranch in Santa Barbara. Eric could get the Lakers involved. Nina works for MTV. I'm sure she could get them to cover it, especially with Topaz involved. You said we needed publicity and money. We need to educate young people and MTV's audience is young people."

The ideas flowed out of her like water. Dr. Nichols looked at her and smiled.

"I've missed you working for me. You were always so creative. No one has ever been able to put together the Christmas parties the way you did."

"Really?" Keisha was surprised by her father's compliment.

"You have a knack for it, baby. That's your gift."

"How come you never told me any of this before?"

"Because I wanted you to have your own life and follow your own dreams."

"I wish you had told me, Daddy. I've been feeling pretty useless ever since Kendra went to school. I was so busy being a wife and a mother, I forgot about myself."

"Don't ever do that, sweetheart. You're much too precious to lose. That's why Eric married you. He fell in love with you. You have to keep yourself alive in a marriage, otherwise you'll slowly begin to die and wake up one day wondering what happened."

Keisha knew there was truth to what her father said because she had never felt more alive. She had been beating herself up for months and the answer was inside her. Suddenly she heard Karla's words the day they had left for California.

"You'll find your purpose out there."

Karla's words had proved themselves true once again.

"I have a name for the foundation." She was so excited she was about to explode. "A Chocolate Affair. Chocolate because this is about black people and an affair is a concern, not some kind of forbidden love relationship." She laughed at the thought and her father laughed with her. "Maybe I better not use that."

"I like it. It's catchy." Dr. Nichols was already writing it on a pad. "When do you want to do it?"

"September," Keisha blurted out after some thought. "For National Sickle Cell Month."

"My daughter is a genius. Now do you think you'll have time to get this thing together? September is only a few months away."

"I'll get my friends to help me. Hey . . . I'll ask Rosalyn, too. Oh, this is too good." She took her father's pad and began jotting down her thoughts. "The hardest thing will be ticket sales. I'll get Eric to get Kobe Bryant to come. Women love him. We'll sell every ticket."

She smiled as the ideas continued to come.

I know God sent me to LA for a reason and I believe this is it.

Chapter Twenty-two

Jade paused to look out of the window at the boats docked in the Marina. It was evening and the harbor was alive with activity from the restaurants and shops. From her penthouse view, people on the boardwalk looked like tiny ants. There was a view of the water from every window in the condo, which was why she and Sean had chosen the high-rise because Sean loved the tranquility of the water.

She placed a marinated steak on the grill and clicked off the rice steamer. She would be having steamed veggies for dinner again. She had five more pounds to lose and she had finally started working out with Nina. After her mother's comments about her weight at Kobe's dedication, she was determined to get back in shape.

She heard the front door close and looked up to see Sean come into the family room with his basketball gear. He flipped on the television and collapsed on the sofa.

"Hi, honey. You're just in time. I grilled a steak for dinner and it's just about done."

She flipped the sizzling meat and placed it on a plate. It was beautifully seared and it smelled delicious. She loved steak and she wanted a slice of it badly, but she was able to resist. She prepared her husband's plate and carried it into the family room on a tray.

"Thanks, baby. I was coming to get it. You didn't have to bring it in here."

She handed him the tray complete with silverware and a glass of juice and returned to the kitchen for her vegetables and water with lemon. She sat on the sofa beside him and sprinkled lemon pepper on her food; it always seemed to make things a little more palatable.

She watched him wolf down his dinner without a word. She knew she had been wrong to refuse him that night he wanted to make love and he hadn't tried since. But he would succumb to her charm tonight. She smiled as she thought about the negligee, massage oil with warm pineapple, and edible mango body gel that Topaz had given her.

"Sean, Kobe has an appointment with the pediatrician tomorrow and I have to teach an art class at the youth center."

"What youth center?" He opened a book and began to read.

"It's an eight-week class for children at a youth center near Crenshaw." She finished her water and wished she had a strawberry soda with crushed ice and a chili dog with extra onions from Pinks. "Will you take him?"

He flipped the book closed and looked at her. "I'm not your baby-sitter. I took him to his last appointment. Aren't you ever going to do anything for your son?"

"All right, Sean. This is not about Kobe. You've been avoiding me ever since I went to Washington. What's wrong?"

"Nothing." He was mumbling like a little boy.

"Yes, there is. What's bothering you, Sean?" Her voice was kind and soft. She moved closer and he jumped up.

"I said nothing, now would you stop nagging me?"

He sounded irritated with her. Sean went into the bedroom and she followed. His exercise clothing was strewn from the bed to the shower. She was looking at him and tripped over his Nikes in the doorway. She was so angry, she picked one up and threw it at him.

"Are you crazy?" The shoe zipped past his head and crashed onto the dresser before it fell on the floor.

"I could have fallen and seriously injured myself on these damn shoes. How many times have I asked you to put away your things?"

"I know you must be crazy throwing shoes at me."

He picked up the shoe she had thrown. He glared at her as he picked up the other.

"You're calling me crazy? You must have lost your damn mind. You won't even talk to me."

"Don't curse at me."

"I'll curse as much as I want, damn it. Do you want to talk or what?"

"Talk about what?"

"What the hell is bothering you."

"Get out of here, Jade, and stop hassling me."

He picked up his dirty sweats and walked into the bathroom and stuffed them in a hamper.

"Hassling you? I'm trying to have a conversation and you say I'm hassling you. You are so ignorant." He had her so frustrated, she was shouting.

"Peace . . . a man needs peace and quiet and I can't get it in my own house. Go in the other room and stop nagging me."

Now he was yelling, too. He had never yelled at her before and that hurt her more than anything. He stood there and watched her cry while she waited for him to come take her in his arms and comfort her. When he didn't come to her aid, she collapsed on the floor and sobbed.

"I gotta get out of here."

He was equally frustrated and hurt. He couldn't stand to see her cry and he was consumed with guilt and didn't know what he should do. He carefully stepped around her and left the bedroom. Moments later, she heard the front door slam.

"Sean . . ." She got up and ran into the living room and opened the front door. The elevator doors had just closed. She wondered how he had gotten an elevator so quickly.

"Oh, my God." She fell on the floor on her hands and knees. "Oh, my God. It hurts, it hurts so bad."

She crawled across the floor back into the bedroom and pulled herself up onto the bed. She lay there crying in a pillow and inhaling his scent.

"He doesn't love me anymore." She was whispering to herself in the dark. The phone rang several times, but she didn't answer it. She didn't want to talk to anyone, especially him.

He doesn't want to make love to me. That's what this is really about.
"Because I'm ugly and fat."

Jade cried all night, miserable, because she thought he no longer found her attractive. She had read about men no longer being attracted to their wives after giving birth, but she never dreamt it would happen to her. She fell asleep with her clothes on.

Kobe woke her up early the following morning. She opened her eyes and was surprised to see that Sean's side of the bed had not been slept in. She went into the baby's room, expecting to find him talking to their son, but found he wasn't there either. She scooped Kobe up and carried him into the kitchen while she heated his formula. Sean wasn't in the family room, or in the living room.

He never came home.

She cried as she quickly bathed the baby, dressed him, and then herself. She had to get out of there. She didn't want to be home when he did return. There was no way she could teach class today, she was a wreck waiting to happen. She strapped Kobe in his car seat and drove toward Bel Air. She had to find Nina.

"I'm on my way over. How do I get there?" Her voice cracked and she fought a battle against the tears.

"Jade?" Nina was not an early riser and Jade had awakened her out of a sound sleep.

"Yes." She choked and coughed.

"Is something wrong? You don't sound right." Nina was fully awake now.

Tears rolled out of Jade's almond eyes and she sniffed. "No."

"There is too something wrong. Where are you?"

"In the car."

She had never had such a difficult time speaking in her life. She started to hang up and drive to a hotel, but she didn't want Sean to find her or the baby ever. If she used a credit card, he would surely track her down. She wanted him to suffer.

"Jade, are you still there?"

"Yes."

"Where are you?"

"At the west gate. How do I get up to the house?"

She had never been to Topaz's house by herself. She had been there with Nina once, but she had no idea how to navigate the twisting, turning roads cut through the hills that led up to the house.

"You stay right there beside the gate. I'm driving down to meet you. I don't want you to get lost."

Jade tried her best to rid herself of any tears before she arrived. Five minutes later Nina made a U-turn in front of her and headed back up the road and finally turned into the sprawling gated estate.

Nina pulled into a stall and Jade parked behind her and rested her head on the steering wheel. Nina tapped on the window. Jade unlocked the door, and Nina climbed in beside her.

"What is going on? Why are you and Kobe out at seven in the morning?"

Jade could see the concern on Nina's face, and her eyes welled up with tears. "We had another fight," she managed through a sob.

"Again?" Nina let out a long sigh, leaned back, and rested her head on the headrest. "What happened this time?"

"I don't know. We were having dinner one minute and fighting the next."

"About what?"

"Nothing really. His clothes on the floor."

"Jade, go home. Go home and apologize. You and Sean have to stop having these silly, stupid fights."

"I can't." She broke down and cried. "I can't."

She was an emotional wreck. She was too embarrassed to tell her best friend, whom every man in town wanted, that her husband was no longer attracted to her.

"Why can't you, Jade?" Nina spoke softly and rubbed her on the back. Jade had never lifted her head from the steering wheel. She couldn't look at Nina.

"He's gone." She was whispering again.

Nina thought Topaz had cornered the drama queen market, but Jade had her by a long shot with this one. But then what she said finally registered. "Sean?"

Jade nodded her head to agree.

"What?" Nina squealed so loudly, she woke the baby.

"He left us, Nina . . . last night, and he never came home."

Chapter Twenty-three

Topaz was so excited she didn't even notice the green Mercedes truck parked in front of the garage as she buckled her daughter in the car seat. She was so happy she had been singing ever since they made the date.

She drove out on Sunset to Pacific Palisades. As she approached the house number, she was suddenly extremely nervous. She pulled over to the side and took several deep breaths.

What if he doesn't like me anymore? What if he doesn't like Turquoise and she doesn't like him?

She had never thought about that before and she was terrified by the idea. So much so, that she almost turned around and drove back to the house, but she knew if she did, Nina would kill her. Germain had said they would take things slowly, and if things didn't work out, he would allow her to have a relationship with their son. That made it a win-win situation, but it did nothing for the butterflies fluttering in her stomach. She took another deep breath and stepped on the gas.

The road curved and suddenly there was a view of the Pacific Ocean. It was a quiet, peaceful neighborhood where all of the estates faced the water. She stopped in front of a pink stucco Spanish-influenced house with a red Mediterranean roof, surrounded by lofty palms. The flawless green lawn was freshly manicured and a myriad of colorful flowers swayed in a gentle breeze.

This is fabulous, Germain, but you always did have good taste.

She led Turquoise by the hand up a redbrick path to the front door. Before she could ring the doorbell, Chris swung it open.

"Mother." She clasped a hand to her mouth as she looked at her son for the first time in three years. He had his father's coloring, which had deepened from the California sun. His hair was darker, too, but the rest was all her. She pulled him into her arms and broke into tears.

"Look at my baby boy. You're all grown up."

"I'm not a baby anymore, Mother. I'm a young man." He smiled Germain's smile and looked at her through sparkling topaz eyes.

"You most certainly are a young man and an extremely hand-some one."

"Is this my baby sister?" He smiled at Turquoise and then at Topaz.

She introduced the two children and then Chris gave her a hug. She looked up and saw Germain standing in the doorway.

"She has eyes like you and me, Mother."

Topaz nodded and smiled at Germain, who came outside and swooped Turquoise up in his arms and tickled her until she was bubbling with laughter.

"Come inside, Mother. I want you to see my new computer."

He took by the hand and led her through the living room and up a winding white staircase and down the hall to a room with bunk beds and NBA bedspreads, curtains, and rugs. There was a huge poster of her in the middle of the wall next to Eric's. Her own topaz eyes seemed to be staring at her and they gave her an eerie feeling.

"See, Mother?" He proudly displayed one of the new computers with push-button Internet access encased in a transparent cover. "I do my school papers, play games, and send e-mail. What's your e-mail address?" He clicked several buttons on the mouse and pulled up a rolodex.

"Topazgirl."

She was glad she had let Nina convince her to purchase a computer, although she had never used it. She watched his fingers swiftly type on the keys. Germain had done an amazing job with him. She hoped things went well today. She looked at Turquoise, who seemed right at home in Germain's arms. They looked like father and daughter. Her little girl needed a man like him in her life . . . they all did.

"We'd better get going if we're going to Disneyland. Chris will try to keep you in his room all day." Germain gave her a quick tour of the rest of the house and they were on their way.

The first thing Chris wanted to do was go to Space Mountain.

"He still remembers the time you brought him here. This is the first time he's been back. I promised him we'd come ever since we moved here and we never did. I guess we needed you." He smiled and she thought she saw him blush as the butterflies in her stomach increased their fluttering.

"I'm glad you waited for Turquoise and me. Now this place will hold special memories for all of us. She's never been here either. Every time I tried to think about bringing her, I couldn't."

He brushed a lock of hair from her face and she smiled.

"Come on, Mommy, I'm riding with you."

Chris slipped his hand in hers and smiled. She felt her heart melting and wondered how she had ever left him, and almost cried. She didn't feel worthy of his adoration. She held his hand and Germain snapped pictures. A woman in line volunteered to take a picture of him and his beautiful family.

Chris was her riding partner for most of the day and Turquoise was equally content with Germain. He bought her a Mickey Mouse and he was her best friend forever. While they were in the gift shop, Chris pointed at a poster of Mickey kissing a blushing Minnie Mouse.

"I want that for my room, Daddy. It reminds me of you and Mother."

"It does?" Germain tried not to laugh. "Why?"

"Because that's how you look when you whisper in Mommy's ear." He giggled and Germain laughed.

"All right, man. I'll get you that poster." He pulled off his Mickey baseball cap and rubbed his head and the two of them searched in the bin for the poster.

Topaz watched Turquoise pull off her brother's cap and rub his head the way Germain had, and laughed.

I want to get something special for Germain as a memento of our day.

She spotted a case with watches and grinned. *Perfect.* She pointed out a really nice gold watch he could wear at his practice. *Now he can think about me whenever he looks at the time.* She stuffed the gift bag in her purse and found Germain and the kids in the front of the store.

"Mother." Chris took her by the hand again. "I've been thinking. You need to go on a ride with Daddy." He was so serious she almost laughed.

"I need to ride with Daddy?" She glanced at Germain and smiled. "Okay, which ride?"

"You choose, Daddy." Germain selected a boat ride and secured the children's belts before he hopped in beside Topaz, who was sitting directly behind them.

"I thought I'd never have a chance to be with you by myself. My son's got it bad."

She laughed and settled back inside the crook of his arm. It had been so long and it felt so right. He handed her a small package from the gift store. "I got you a little something."

She smiled and took the box. Things were going even better than she hoped. She quickly removed the paper and gasped when she saw the charm bracelet.

"I love it, Germain."

He took the bracelet out and fastened it around her wrist. "It's fourteen-karat gold. I know how picky you are."

145

"Oh, Germain. I'm not that girl anymore. I wouldn't care if it was plastic. You gave this to me and I'll never take it off." She kissed him before she had a chance to think about it and he smiled.

"I got something for you, too." She reached inside her purse and handed him the bag. "I'm not as good as you. I didn't have time to get yours wrapped."

He tore into the bag with the energy of a child and grinned when he pulled out the Mickey Mouse watch. "I'll wear it every day, pretty girl." He leaned over and gave a wonderful kiss that left her breathless.

Pretty girl . . . He called me pretty girl. She secretly wiped the tears from her eyes as they got out of the boat.

The children fell asleep as soon as they were out of the parking lot. Topaz rubbed the coarse black hairs on the back of Germain's hand.

"I had a wonderful time, Dr. Gradney." She leaned over and kissed him on the cheek.

"I had a great time too, Ms. Black." She smiled when she heard him use her maiden name, and as they rode in silence, she enjoyed the way his favorite fragrance combined with his body scent.

"Turquoise will never be the same. That little girl definitely has a thing for you. I was almost jealous." She laughed at the thought.

"I feel you. I'm sure glad her brother allowed me to have one ride with my woman. Dang . . . I thought I was going to have to knock the little dude out."

"Germain, you are so crazy. I can't believe what you just said."

They held hands and chatted all the way back to his house. Topaz felt like a teenager.

"So when can I see you again, Ms. Black?" He smiled as he cut off her truck.

"I don't know, Dr. Gradney, when would you like to see me again?" She couldn't be more pleased that he had already invited her on a second date.

"I have tickets to a play on Sunday. How about I pick you up for dinner and we go out, just you and me, no kids?" He looked in the back at Chris, who was sound asleep, and Topaz laughed.

"That sounds great, Germain. I can't wait."

"You've changed, pretty girl, and I'm loving the new you."

She kissed Germain and then Chris after Germain woke him up.

"I'll send you an e-mail, Mommy. I love you."

She looked at Germain, who only raised an eyebrow, and she pulled off, savoring the moment.

My son just told me he loved me for the very first time. She felt the tears well up and let them flow. "Thanks, God, and thank you for Keisha."

Her cell phone rang and she answered it expecting to hear Nina.

"Keisha, I was just thinking about you. I just got back from Disneyland. We had the most wonderful time and we're going out again on Sunday."

"That's wonderful, T. I'm so happy for you."

"Thanks, Keisha. I don't know if this would ever have happened if it wasn't for you and God."

"I told you prayer works. Speaking of which, Jade needs a lot. Sean left her."

"He did what?" Topaz almost dropped the phone.

"They had a big fight last night and he walked out. She's at your house. Nina called and told me."

"Oh, my God. That's terrible." She had forgotten all about her interlude with Sean for the day as waves of fresh guilt flooded her mind.

"It sure is."

"Do you know what they fought about?"

"Nina said it was over his shoes, but something's been brewing for a while. Eric's been trying to find Sean."

"Gosh, I hope everything's okay." Topaz turned up the air conditioner. She had broken into a sweat.

"Me too. I want details."

Topaz clicked off the phone and rubbed her hand through her head.

Sean left Jade. . . . I hope he doesn't tell anyone what happened.

She looked at her charm bracelet and suddenly she was angry. "I've waited a long time to see my family back together . . . and I'm not going to let Jade spoil it because she can't keep her man."

Chapter Twenty-four

Nina clicked a button on the mouse and smiled when she heard the computer say, "You've got mail." There had been a message from Kyle every day since they met at the ranch. She scanned the list of unopened mail for "twincity," the address he had created for his personal messages.

He always sent her his plans for the day, and a funny story about something he had done. They were so crazy that Nina secretly wondered if Kyle made them up. Whether they were true or not, she loved them and looked forward to his nightly call when they would laugh nonstop for over an hour.

Nina was surprised when she got to the bottom of the list and didn't see a message from him. She knew she had missed it so she scanned the list a second time and found nothing. Disappointed, she clicked off her computer and stared at the blank screen.

I guess he finally got bored with me. Jade said he never kept a girlfriend long. All that talk about marrying me. I actually believed him. That's what I get for being stupid.

Their whirlwind romance had lasted two weeks. She closed the computer and went into the room next to her where Jade was still asleep. The crib next to her was empty. Turquoise's nanny, Rosa, who loved babies, had instantly fallen in love with Kobe. She had come for him the moment he opened his almond eyes and cried.

"Jade." She sat on the bed next to her and shook her friend gently. "It's a beautiful day. Let's do something."

Jade pulled the covers over her head and rolled over. It was Saturday and she had been in bed for two days and refused to eat. Nina had heard her crying off and on. She remembered how Topaz had taken to her bed when she found out Germain had been living in Los Angeles for months and she knew nothing about it.

If this is what love does to people, I want no part of it. No one is ever going to have that much control over me.

Nina went downstairs to the gym and found Topaz running on the treadmill. Glass walls gave them a view of the pool and tennis courts. She did a few stretches and climbed on the stationary bicycle. Topaz waved and continued running.

"Good morning, Mrs. Gradney." She couldn't help laughing when Topaz jumped off the treadmill and started dancing. "You are so silly."

She collapsed on the floor in front of Nina. "You broke my concentration."

"I did not. You've got it so bad after one date, you know you were concentrating on Germain, so how could I break your concentration?"

"I know, huh." Topaz grinned and stood in front of a mirror inspecting her figure. "I wish my stomach was a little flatter."

"It'll get there when you start belly rubbing with Germain."

"Belly rubbing? You are sick." She laughed as she sat down on the bench to do her upper-body work. "We're taking things slowly."

"Right." Nina peddled away on the bicycle. "The only reason you guys didn't do the wild thang was that there were children present. You'll get some tomorrow. You've been without some for too long."

Nina was surprised when Topaz had no further comment. They exercised in silence for several minutes.

"How's Jade?" Topaz finally asked.

"In the same state you were in when you saw Germain at the clinic."

"Poor thing." Topaz pulled and released the weights.

"After being around the two of you I don't ever want to be in love. That is too much pain. I don't like pain."

"I know, but it's the best thing there is when it's right. You'll see."

"No, I won't." Nina jumped off the bike and picked up a pair of free weights. She knew how badly she had felt over missed e-mail. She just wanted all those feelings to disappear as quickly as they had come. She heard a tap on the glass beside her and looked up to see Manuel, one of the security guards, standing at the door with an envelope. She put down the weights and opened the door.

"Miss Nina, there was a telegram for you." She thanked him and felt her heart race when she realized it was from Kyle. She quickly opened it and began to read.

Nina,

If I'm correct, you should be finishing up your workout right about now. It's Saturday and I want to see my favorite girl tonight. When we spoke the other night, you said you didn't have plans, so I'm hoping you'll join me this weekend. There's a flight from LAX to JFK at noon and you have a seat. The limo will arrive at ten-thirty. Get some sleep on the plane because we're going dancing.

Kyle

"Kyle wants me to come to New York tonight to go dancing." Topaz let the weights drop. "You're kidding. Are you going?"

"Should I?" She couldn't believe she was even considering it, but she wanted to see him.

"Do you really want me to answer that? You've been glowing ever since you came back from Santa Barbara."

"He's sending a limo to pick me up at ten-thirty." She couldn't contain her smile. She looked at her watch and screamed. "It's nine-thirty."

"You'd better get going." Topaz smiled at her as she headed for the door.

"I can't go." Nina stopped and turned around, the smile missing from her pretty face. "I have to stay here with Jade."

"Jade doesn't appear to be leaving her bed any time soon. If she needs anything, I'll be around. You go have a good time."

"Thanks, Topaz. And thanks for being so nice to Jade."

She dashed up the stairs, showered, and tossed items into a suitcase. She had just tucked her favorite black dress in a garment bag, when security notified her that her driver was waiting. She went into Jade's room.

"I'll be in New York for a few days with Kyle. He wants to take me dancing." She almost felt guilty for being so happy when Jade was so miserable. She sat up and looked at Nina.

"Is it okay if I stay here?" She looked terrible. Her hair was tangled and her eyes were red. She hadn't showered or brushed her teeth.

"Sure, honey. Topaz wants you to. And the baby is fine. Rosa is wonderful. She could take care of my kids any day if I ever had some." She kissed her on the forehead. "Call me on my cell if you need me."

"I won't and please don't tell Kyle anything about us. I don't know if Sean said anything to his family, but I don't want them in my business." She sank back in the bed and disappeared under the covers.

Nina dashed downstairs to the limo. "Don't do what I would do," Topaz called as she ran out of the house.

She thought about Topaz and Jade all the way to the airport and then wondered if she was doing the right thing as she buckled her seat in first class.

A man doesn't send you a first-class ticket to New York and not expect something in return. Kyle is taking this relationship to another level. He's going to want me to have sex with him.

For the first time in her life Nina was terrified. She had never been one to take sex casually. She felt it required some sort of a commitment. The thought of being with Kyle thrilled her, but she didn't know how serious he was. She had never experienced what she was feeling now with any man before, and she didn't want to get hurt.

In the past, if a guy hinted about sex before she had a chance to get to know him, she immediately lost interest. Now here she was flying across the country to God knows what. Kyle had told her the first night that he wasn't Sean, and she had promptly replied, she wasn't Jade. *I should have kept my big mouth shut.*

She was amazed she had fallen asleep when the flight attendant woke her for their arrival in New York City. Kyle was waiting when she walked into the terminal.

"Hey, you."

He smiled and she felt her insides beginning to turn into butter, like a schoolgirl with her first crush.

"I'm so glad you came."

Those Ross brothers and that irresistible smile. It was more deadly than any weapon.

"Hi, Kyle." She knew she was blushing, something she never did, and relaxed when his hand slid into hers. Suddenly she knew everything would be all right and she felt safe.

They chatted about nothing in particular all the way to his loft in Soho.

"Sean lived here when he was playing for the Concordes. He really fixed this place up. He sold it to me when he moved to California."

Nina looked at the iron staircase, resembling a fire escape, winding up in the center of the warehouse-type structure. The kitchen, living, and dining rooms were on the first level. An entertainment room, office, guest bedroom, and bath were on the second level. The stairs ended on the third floor. The entire level was his bedroom and bath. She noticed he had left her things in the bedroom on the second level.

"I thought we'd order in something for dinner, get dressed, and then we'll go check out some clubs and do a little dancing." He did a little step and she laughed.

They ordered some of the best fettuccine and pizza she had ever eaten. He brought up a bottle of Cristal and champagne glasses and smiled as he popped the cork.

"This isn't that bottle of champagne I told you about." He gave her a mischievous look as he poured it into their glasses and Nina couldn't help laughing.

"Where is it?"

"In a very special place, awaiting that special moment." He raised an eyebrow.

"You are sick." She shook her head and laughed. "You missed your calling. You should have been a comedian."

"Maybe I'll retire and give it a try." He touched his glass to hers and they both drank.

"Are you serious?" Sometimes she couldn't tell if he was teasing or not.

"Yes."

"Really?"

"I could retire and never have to work another day in my life, but I was teasing about the comedy."

"You can retire at thirty-two?" Jade had mentioned that he was the financial whiz of the family and had advised everyone on investing.

"Sure, I could. But I'd get bored. So until I find something else I'd like to do, I'll keep my job." He poured more champagne into their glasses.

"That's really great, Kyle." She smiled and he kissed her.

"So are you, Nina Beaubien."

He kissed her again and she knew she would have to make love to this man, even if he did break her heart. It was a risk worth taking.

"Let's get dressed. I could sit here and talk to you all night long, but I invited you to go dancing."

Neither one of them moved.

"We don't have to go out," she heard herself say.

"I know, but if we stay here, I'll want to do a lot more than just talk."

"That's okay with me."

Nina couldn't believe what she had just said. She wanted to say it was the champagne, but it was him. He had her saying and doing things she had never done before. She had it so bad, she felt herself shaking and she was so embarrassed. She didn't want him to think she was immature. He pulled her into his arms and kissed her. Suddenly she was standing on her feet and he gently pushed her toward her room.

"I'll meet you back in here in an hour. Is that enough time for you?"

She nodded and he disappeared up the stairs while she was trying to figure out what just happened. A warm shower revived her and settled her thoughts. When she stepped out of the bedroom, he was sitting there waiting. He whistled, and she blushed.

"Nina, baby, you are so sweet. You're like a bag of cookies or a big box of chocolate candy. I could be greedy and gobble up everything. . . . I used to do that when I was a kid. But I'm a man now and I've learned that taking my time and enjoying each bite only heightens the flavor."

Most guys would have been all over her by now. If she had been with Jamil, they would never have left the house. He would have taken his fill and been asleep by now. Now she understood that Jamil was a boy, Kyle was a man.

They went to three clubs . . . salsa, hip-hop, and old school. Kyle was an excellent dancer. They had the most fun remembering the old dances they used to do. Kyle made her laugh so hard, her stomach hurt. The sun was just about to rise when they returned to the loft.

After brunch at Steve Baldwin's, they went to the art museum, held hands and walked in Central Park, then back to the loft to change for dinner at Bea Smith's, after which, they went to see the *Lion King.*

He took her to breakfast before her flight back to LA at noon. Neither one of them wanted her to get on the airplane. He kissed her good-bye and she fought back the tears until she got on the plane, where she cried for over an hour. Finally, she dialed Topaz's cell number and was so glad when her cousin answered the phone.

"I think I love him," she sobbed into the telephone. Now she understood why Topaz and Jade had taken to their beds. If it felt this good to be in love, being out of it must be absolutely horrible.

"Did you give him some?" That was usually her favorite question for Topaz.

"No. . . ." She felt like a three-year-old little girl, sniffing and blowing her nose inside the rest room. She was a mess. She was glad she had come inside.

"And you're this messed up? Dang, girl, what did he do to you?"

She cried a fresh batch of tears as she relived her weekend through a series of flashbacks, remembering all the places he had taken her and the things he had said. She sniffed and blew her nose.

"All that, huh?"

Nina finally laughed. "How was your date with Germain?"

"I'm the one who should be crying. It was absolutely incredible. We did everything I told you not to do and what you didn't do."

"You made love?" Nina wiped her last tear.

"Yes, girl. We got a room at the Bel Air hotel and did it all night long. I just got in."

"What?" Nina screamed, hoping no one had heard her. "I thought you guys were taking things slow?"

"We are . . . that's why we're not getting married until next year."

"You guys are getting married again?" Nina was whispering on the phone.

"Yes, girl. I could hardly believe it myself. Germain and I are getting married. He wants to adopt Turquoise, too. Things couldn't be more perfect."

"Yeah, girl. I feel you." She looked at the photos they had dropped at One-Hour Photo while they were having breakfast. "Everything is perfect."

Chapter Twenty-five

Keisha thought she was dreaming when she heard the unfamiliar sound of rain pelting the Atlantic Ocean on the roads of the vineyard. She lay in bed enjoying the smell of the damp earth mingled with ocean air when Eric entered the bedroom carrying a tray with hot tea, and a plate of waffles with warm strawberry syrup and whipped cream.

"Good morning, beautiful wife." She sat up and he set the tray down on the bed in front of her and grinned. "I made the tea just the way you like it and these are Sarah's homemade waffles. She made them especially for you since we're going back to LA tonight."

"I'm not ready to go home. I wish we could stay here forever listening to this wonderful rain. I didn't realize how much I missed it."

He climbed into bed next to her and cut a bite of the waffle and fed it to her. She chewed slowly, savoring the mixture of flavors on her tongue.

"That is so good. What did I ever do to deserve you?"

"Put up with me and my madness and still manage to treat me like a king."

"I love you and your madness." She kissed him gently on the lips and ate some more of the waffle.

"Your lips taste good . . . like strawberry syrup and whipped cream. I'll have to remember that." His honey eyes sparkled as he kissed her again.

"You are so bad." Keisha laughed. "But I'll get the syrup as soon as we get back." She picked up the cup of tea. "You eat the rest of this, sweetie, although I know you already had four of them with bacon and scrambled eggs with cheese before you brought this one up."

"You know me too well." He smiled as he finished the last of the waffle. "I never thought I'd be able to be like this with anyone."

"Be like what?" Her eyes searched his face as she sipped her favorite apple tea sweetened with cinnamon and brown sugar.

"So comfortable, free, able to talk about stuff. But when I saw that big booty, I knew I could tell you anything."

She smacked him with a pillow and he fell out of the bed and onto the floor, laughing.

"You are so sick." Keisha watched him pull himself back up onto the bed, admiring his nicely cut chest and six-pack, and smooth skin that tasted and looked like honey.

"You are so fine, baby." She thought she saw him blushing as a smile lit up his face.

"Can you believe Kyle? He couldn't stop grinning all night. Your girl sure did a number on him. Kirk said he's never seen him act this way about anyone."

"The bigger they come, the harder they fall. Nina's beautiful, sweet, and smart. I hope things work out for them. Topaz's producer, Jamil, gave her a ring, but she wouldn't marry him. She likes being single."

"So does Kyle. That's probably why they get along so well. Some girl is always trying to marry him. "

"I just want all of our friends to be as happy as we are. I'm so happy for Germain and Topaz. They get together and then Sean and Jade fall apart. Did the twins mention anything about Sean?"

"Nope. Nina told Kyle about it and she made him promise he wouldn't tell anyone. Those twins can't keep a secret; he'll break soon. If one knows, they both know."

"And men say women gossip. You guys gossip just as much if not more."

"That may be true, luscious lips, but I never tell anything you tell me." He stretched and smiled at her.

"That's because you're special and an exception to every rule and I'd kick your butt if you did."

"Flattery and promises will get you everything. Are you sure you want to go home tonight? Don't you love it here? No phones, no television, a cook, the ocean, and this wonderful big bed."

"You are so bad." Keisha giggled. "I want to stay, too, but we have to get started on the foundation. We're having a meeting at the house tomorrow, remember?"

"I remember and I know how important this is to you."

The next evening Topaz and Germain arrived grinning and holding hands, followed by Nina, who was glowing, and Jade. It was the first time she had left the house in weeks.

"Now that Sean is gone she stays home." Eric and Keisha were whispering in the kitchen while they prepared the beverages.

"Whatever happened, it's not all her fault."

Topaz walked in crunching a carrot. "I'm hungry, Key. Where's the real food? I know you got some Thai food or something up in here."

"We have food but no one's eating until after the meeting."

Keisha handed Topaz another carrot and passed out the drinks. She was just about to begin the presentation when Rosalyn arrived. Topaz gave her a dirty look, but she pretended not to notice. She introduced Rosalyn, who presented the group with the medical information about sickle cell disease.

"I can't believe she invited us over to depress us. That's all I need." Keisha overheard Jade whispering to Nina.

"All of us in this room are extremely blessed." Keisha looked directly at Jade as she continued speaking. "I've asked you all here because you are my friends and we need your help. One year at our annual Christmas party a little boy expressed concern over the lack of participation by African-American celebrities in televised events for this cause. So I'd like to do an affair that no one will ever forget and raise money for research."

"I'll do a concert," Topaz offered. "I'll get the record company to give us CDs and posters and buy a big ad in the souvenir book."

"The souvenir book." Keisha looked directly at Topaz. "How could I ever forget?"

"I'll be in charge of the book," Nina offered.

"I was hoping you'd be our producer and put together the show for the concert."

"Me? A producer?" Nina was shocked. "Okay. I'll ask Kyle to do the book. I'm sure he'll be able to get you lots of corporate sponsors."

"I talked to some of my boys in the NBA. We'll be very happy to do a celebrity basketball game." Eric grinned at his wife.

"That is so wonderful, baby. I can't believe you didn't say anything to me." Keisha kissed him on the lips and everybody said aah.

"I am the cochairman of this event and I can keep a secret, too."

"You sure can. You go, boy, with your bad self." Keisha grinned and Jade let out a long sigh.

"We can put together an opposing team of musicians, actors, and athletes, do something like a rock-and-jock classic," Nina suggested.

"See, that's why you're the producer," Eric yelled excitedly.

Everyone buzzed with ideas and volunteered for various tasks except Jade, who remained silent and picked at her nails.

"Jade, we need two things that only you can help us with."

Everyone was silent as Keisha looked at Jade. "We need an art poster that we could sell. Will you paint us one?"

"What's the second thing?"

"We'd like to have the concert at your ranch. It's invitation only," Keisha finished, and everyone looked at Jade and waited for her answer.

"You did this to embarrass me, Keisha. You know Sean and I aren't together and you did this to humiliate me in front of everybody."

"Jade . . ." Nina tried to calm her down, but Jade had a crazed look in her eyes.

"I can't stand you. You're just little Miss Perfect with your perfect, boring life. Your life is so perfect you have to try and save the rest of the world so everybody can be perfect and boring just like you. You're so good at everything; you draw your own damn art poster, and as for the ranch, ask Sean yourself. I know you've spoken to him."

Everyone was stunned as Jade jumped up and headed for the door.

"No, she didn't . . ." Topaz began.

"No, Topaz. This is my house. I'll handle this one," Eric said. Keisha had never seen him so upset.

"Jade, you are my best friend's wife, but no one comes in my house and talks to my wife any kind of way. No one is trying to embarrass you. You just embarrassed yourself. For some reason you've had it out for Keisha ever since we moved here. Keisha has done nothing but try to be your friend. Sean and I wanted you guys to be friends because we were friends. I've seen my wife almost in tears because she didn't know what she had done to make you dislike her so much. And Sean . . ."

"Sean!" Jade screamed. "It's always about Sean and what Sean wants. Sean wants me to be a wife like Keisha and Karla. Sean wants me to stay home. Sean wants a baby. Sean wants me to use his name. Sean wants to go visit his family. Well, I tried to do everything that Sean wanted and he's gone. He's gone."

She collapsed on Eric and Nina. The sobs came from deep within her soul.

"I don't think she's been eating," Nina explained. "If I had known she was going to act like this, I would never have brought her. I'm sorry, you guys." Nina's face was wet with tears.

"It's okay, Nina." Eric looked as if he wanted to cry, too.

"She's really hurting." Keisha handed Nina tissues as she wiped the tears from her own eyes. "Has she been talking?"

Nina shook her head no. "I try to get her to talk about it, but she won't. She thinks Sean left her because he's not attracted to her."

"Poor baby." Keisha sniffed and pulled another tissue from the box.

Eric handed them all cups of tea, made the way Keisha liked it. Topaz and Germain sat in the living room talking quietly. Rosalyn had left, unnoticed.

"I don't think she meant those things, Keisha." Nina looked up at her when Jade went into the bathroom to throw up.

"She's been through a lot. They should have had some counseling before things got so out of hand." Keisha handed Nina an ice pack. "Take this to her. And see if you can get her to lie down in the guest room."

Nina got up to go to the bathroom. She paused and turned to face Keisha and Eric. "You guys are amazing. I don't know what I would have done if someone had acted like that in my house. Instead of throwing her out, you invite her to stay. I've never known anyone like you. And, Eric, the way you stood up for Keisha, man . . . even I was jealous. I sure hope I can find a man who'll stand up like that for me."

"You will, Nina. You will." Keisha smiled as Topaz entered the room. Eric pulled his wife into his arms.

"You okay, baby?" She nodded and sent him into the living room with Germain.

"Why didn't you throw her out?" Topaz demanded once they were alone. "Girlfriend was seriously player-hating up in here."

"I'm her friend and a friend is always supposed to show love. There are chicken enchiladas in the oven and guacamole and salsa in the fridge. Fix some for yourself and Germain."

"Look at you, still being the hostess. Jade was right. You are perfect." Topaz took the food out and found some plates. "We can all learn how to be a better wife, a better mother, and a better friend from you. I know I have."

"I'm not perfect," Keisha whispered as fresh tears streamed out of her eyes. "Just forgiven."

Chapter Twenty-six

Jade sat in her studio at the ranch staring at the spot where the horizon kissed the ocean. It was an enigma how the two never met, set in perpetual motion by the Creator of the heavens and the earth. She had come there in search of solace and peace, and most importantly herself. She didn't know who she was anymore and that frightened her, especially since she hated the person she had become.

She still couldn't believe the things she had said and done at Keisha and Eric's house that awful night. Thoughts she had kept inside for months had festered and exploded. She could still see the look on Eric's face when she had attacked Keisha. It might have been easier if they had been unkind to her, but they had only shown her love.

Jade had blamed Keisha for excelling where she fell short. She always felt so small around Keisha, but it wasn't Keisha, it was God's love oozing out of her that convicted Jade and instead of trying to be the best she could be, she just resented Keisha.

She still couldn't put all the pieces of that night together. She remembered waking up in Topaz's guest room early the next morning. She had gathered up Kobe's things and hers and left before

Nina or Topaz awakened, picked up the nanny, and driven to Santa Barbara. That had been a month ago. She had sat on the beach for hours crying and talking to God. On other days she would put on music and dance for hours, or she painted.

In the shower, she heard the telephone ringing and picked it up for the first time since she had been there, thinking it might be Nina. She had several messages from Nina and Keisha had even called once. She had missed her friend and was ready to talk to someone besides herself. Jade was surprised when she heard Karla's voice.

"You've been on my heart so strong. I just wanted to know how you are."

"I'm okay." Jade was relieved when she didn't feel a prick of irritation. She was actually glad to hear from Karla.

"God's been healing you. There are some people you must see and something you must do to complete your healing."

"I know." Jade felt a tear slide down her cheek. She didn't think she had any left to cry.

"I'll talk to you soon."

God had Karla call to confirm the things He had told her to do. She wanted to have a girlfriend day at the ranch for Keisha, Nina, and Topaz. She owed each of them an apology.

"Ni-Ni." She was using Turquoise's pronunciation.

"Jade . . . are you okay, honey? We've all been so worried about you."

"I'm fine. I just needed to take some time and get my head together. I've been at the ranch."

"I know. I drove up there and saw your truck in the driveway."

"You're too much. I love you. I want to have a girlfriend day. Do you think you can get Keisha and Topaz to come?"

"The three of us will be there with bells on."

Jade spared no expense and paid strict attention to every minute detail for her party for four. She pored over women's magazines for ideas for her day of healing and pampering. She hadn't realized how much they all had become a part of her life until she pushed them away, even Sean. She needed their friendship, strength, and support.

The doorbell rang and she was immediately nervous. She took a deep breath and tiptoed to the door, hoping they hadn't changed their minds and left. She pulled the door open and eyes met eyes. She felt a lump in her throat and tears on her face.

"I'm so sorry, Keisha, for all the awful things I said that night. Can you ever forgive me?"

That was not the way Jade had planned things, but one will always manage to speak the things hidden inside the heart.

"Of course I do."

Keisha was crying and Nina joined in while Topaz opened a bottle of champagne and poured each of them a glass.

"I think we need a drink." Topaz passed out the glasses while the criers sniffed and wiped the last of their tears. Jade caught sight of the marquis diamond rock on her ring finger.

"What is that? You just blinded me."

"Miss T got herself engaged." Keisha smiled at Topaz.

"To Germain?" A huge grin lit up Jade's face as Topaz nodded.

"Congratulations. Oh, I know how badly you wanted that to happen. I'm so happy for you." Jade kissed her on the cheek and tears filled Topaz's amber eyes.

"All right, cuz. I hope you didn't think you were going to be the only one up in here without mascara running down her eyes." Nina made a face at her cousin and the others laughed.

"Let's have a toast." Jade lifted her glass. "To friendship."

"To love," Topaz added.

"To sisterhood." Keisha smiled.

"Fine men and good sex," Nina finished and tapped her glass to the others. Topaz almost choked and Keisha spat hers out.

"Nina," everyone chorused together.

"That's from hanging out with Kyle." Keisha laughed. "He's a wild one."

"Did you give him some yet?" Topaz demanded. Jade's eyes grew wide and she clasped a hand to her mouth.

"Why are y'all trying to get all up in my business like that?"

Nina walked over to a table of fruit and assorted hot oriental appetizers. A cook brought out freshly prepared sushi and tempura.

"Because we want to know." Topaz followed her to the table and made herself a plate. "This looks great, Jade."

"No, we didn't do it yet. . . ." Nina gave them an impish grin. "And I can't wait to jump that fine man's bones."

They went outside on the deck, where they were served lunch. Jade instructed the waiter to bring them more champagne.

"I got the right kind, didn't I, Topaz? You always get Cristal?"

"Oh, yes." Keisha jumped up and began imitating Topaz. "Waiter, I'd like a bottle of Cristal." The others cried with laughter.

"That's her. That's her." Tears streamed out of Nina's eyes.

"None of you need to laugh." Topaz tried to be serious. "I may order it, but I never see none of you turning it down. Especially you, Jade." Topaz made one of her faces and Keisha got up and ran to the bathroom.

"True dat." Nina laughed. "I remember the night I first met you. Girlfriend had herself a glass, big belly and all. My doctor said it was okay for me to have a sip."

"Right," they chorused.

"You guys are wrong. But that's okay. I love you anyway. That's why I ordered massages, scrubs, and facials for us."

"That was so sweet, Jade." Nina tried not to laugh.

"Keep it up and I'll send the ladies home who came to do our nails and toes."

There was a basket for each of them with a journal, pen, disposable camera, and photo album.

"I thought we'd get together once a year for an annual girlfriend day. No matter where we are, we'll get together, just the four of us, to play," Jade explained.

"Oh, yes," Keisha agreed. "No husbands and children allowed. It'll be just our time to indulge. This was a wonderful idea, Jade."

"I got everyone pajamas, too. There's movies, ice cream, and popcorn for tonight."

"You go, Oprah." Nina kissed her on the cheek.

Jade hadn't been this happy for a long time. She finally felt ready to talk about Sean.

"Have you heard from him at all?" Keisha asked. They were camped out in front of the big-screen TV eating banana splits.

"No. But I wasn't ready to talk to him. I spent a lot of time praying and the Lord showed me a lot of areas where I was wrong. I let the enemy sabotage my marriage." Jade was candid and honest with the ladies.

"God's going to fix everything." Keisha's words were reassuring. "Sean definitely hears from God."

"Yeah," Topaz agreed. "Germain told me he never wanted to see me again ever in life. But Keisha prayed with me and I wrote him a letter and I apologized. If God can put us back together, God can do anything."

"Let's pray for Sean and Jade," Keisha suggested as she took Jade's and Topaz's hands. "Prayer for our marriages should definitely be part of girlfriend day."

"Let's pray for all of our marriages, children, and relationships. Nina, do you want us to pray for you and Kyle?" Topaz smiled at her cousin. "I think you love him," she added softly and Nina blushed.

"What was that?" Jade looked at Topaz.

"Ni-Ni calling me from the airplane."

"I knew it." Jade grinned. "Ni-Ni's gonna be my sister-in-law," she whispered softly as the ladies bowed their heads.

Chapter Twenty-seven

Topaz stood in front of the mirror in the exercise room half-heartedly stretching to tracks from one of her latest songs for the new CD. She loved the song with its hip-hop flavor, and played it every day for her entire workout session.

She barely noticed the music as she practically walked into the mirrored wall, trying to get a better glimpse of her body in the well-lit room. She heard a door slam and almost jumped out of her skin, bumping her forehead on the mirror.

"Got a little extra junk in your trunk, huh?" Nina walked in eating a bagel smothered with cream cheese.

"You scared me." Topaz rolled her eyes at her cousin, turned sideways in front of the mirror, and continued her inspection.

"What are you doing?" Nina popped the last bite in her mouth and stood beside Topaz in front of the mirror.

"Do I look fat?" Topaz turned and faced Nina.

"Oh, my God . . . no." She yelled over the music in order to be heard. "Why are you tripping?"

"Are you sure?" Topaz demanded. "Look closer. What about my stomach?"

Nina sighed loudly. "This is what I get for coming in here while

170

you were still here." She walked around Topaz, carefully looking her up and down. "Your butt's bigger and you do look a little thick around the waist. You'd better stop eating all that fattening food with Germain and Chris."

"I knew it. Oh, my God, what am I going to do?" Topaz collapsed on a chair and cried her eyes out.

Nina looked at her as if she were crazy. "Topaz, what is wrong with you? I can't believe you're acting like this over a few pounds."

"Okay." Topaz sniffed and blew her nose. "I don't know what to do. I have to tell someone before I go crazy and you're the only person I can really trust."

"Tell me what?" Nina watched Topaz pace the floor, wringing her hands. "Topaz . . . you're scaring me." Nina led her outside by the pool to a table with a colorful umbrella. "Now talk."

Topaz looked around the pool area to be absolutely sure they were alone before she finally whispered, "I'm pregnant." She glanced behind them to be sure no one had joined them unexpectedly since her announcement.

"You're pregnant? Is that all?" Nina sighed with relief. "The way you were acting I thought something was really wrong. You and Germain are getting married in June. When's the baby due?"

"In March."

"Perfect. The baby can come to the wedding and you'll look fabulous in your gown. I can't believe you were freaking out over that. But then you are the Drama Queen." Nina looked at Topaz and laughed.

"No." Topaz lowered her voice. "You don't understand." Tears appeared in her amber eyes.

"Understand what?" Nina looked at her, waiting for an answer.

Topaz opened her mouth to speak, but no words came out. All of a sudden, Nina's eyes grew wide with horror.

"This *is* Germain's baby, isn't it?"

"I don't know." Topaz glanced up at Nina out of one eye.

"You don't know?" Nina screamed. "How could you not know

unless . . . Oh, my God. Oh, my God." Nina composed herself and looked at Topaz, who looked down at the table.

"Who else did you sleep with?"

"It only happened one time."

"Who, Topaz?"

"I never meant for it to happen." Topaz looked just like Turquoise when she was being scolded.

"Who, Topaz? Who?" Nina yelled.

"It was Sean, all right? Sean. I slept with Sean. Now you know. Okay?" Topaz sank back into the chair. She pressed her fingers to her temples. She had a throbbing headache and she thought her head would explode. She pulled her hair out of the ponytail and took several deep breaths.

Nina shook her head, shocked, amazed, and unable to believe what she had just heard. "How could you?"

"I told you I never meant for it to happen." She felt nauseated as beads of sweat formed around her hairline.

"Do you really hate Jade that much?" Nina was overly calm. She just didn't have the energy to fight with Topaz anymore about Jade.

"I don't hate Jade," Topaz whispered. She had been wrong to think Nina would understand. Nina was Jade's best friend. She wished she could retract her words, but it was too late now.

"You've done some really mean things, Topaz, but I never thought you would stoop this low. You think you know a person, but we never really know anyone. And you pretended to be her friend . . ."

"Yes, I'm a horrible person. I've hated myself ever since it happened. It was just one night and it didn't mean anything, so there's no way I'm not going to let it ruin my plans with Germain. We are getting married." She paused to look at the huge diamond ring on her finger and then at Nina, who made her feel guilty. "I tried to stay away from Jade and you kept taking me around her . . ."

"So now this is my fault. You are unbelievable."

"Well, it's not my fault that Jade can't keep her man." She rolled her eyes at Nina.

"Sean left Jade because of you." Nina looked at Topaz as she started putting pieces of the puzzle together. "Jade blamed herself and it was you . . ."

"I tried to help her."

"I'd think you of all people would have understood. You know how it feels to want someone so badly."

Topaz cried crocodile tears. "Something was wrong. Sean was unhappy and lonely and sad because she was out of town and . . ."

"And you took advantage."

"No, it wasn't like that at all. I tried to help. I tried to make him understand how important her work was to her, and what a woman needs from a man. "

"So you gave him a little demonstration."

"No . . . we were two old friends just having a conversation. We were both feeling pretty rejected and we were both extremely vulnerable. We should never have been alone. I wish I could do it all over, but I can't. I can't." She put her head on the table and sobbed and a tiny piece of Nina's heart melted. She really did appear to be sorry.

"How in the world do you get yourself into these situations?" For some reason, Nina believed her. It took two to tango. Sean had obviously been a consenting adult. "So what are we going to do?" Nina moved to the chair beside her cousin and smoothed her hair.

"We?" Topaz lifted her head and looked at Nina.

"We. . . . You know I'll help you. We're sisters. I must be crazy but I'm doing this for Jade, too. I want her to work things out with Sean. They're talking again, but they still have a long way to go before they can live as husband and wife again."

"I want them back together, too. He told me how much he loved her. . . . I'll do anything to help Jade. I really do like her, especially after girlfriend day."

"Girlfriend day was nice. . . . So whose baby do you think this is?" Nina shook her head. "I never thought we'd have a conversation like this. That is so ghetto, not knowing who your baby's daddy is."

"In my heart, I know it's Germain's." Topaz nervously fingered a curl in her waist-length hair.

"Girl, you probably turned poor little Sean out. How far apart were these torrid nights of passionate lovemaking?"

"About a week."

"A week? Dang, girl."

"It had to be close if I can't determine whose it is." Topaz held her head in her hands. "Let's go inside. I need an aspirin for my headache."

They stretched out on Nina's bed. She took out her lockbox and opened it and Topaz tried to peek inside.

"Where's that big diamond?" She stuck her hand in the metallic box and Nina slapped it.

"I gave it back to Jamil a long time ago." Nina took the box out on the deck. "Between you and Jade, I will never get married, never have kids, and never have sex."

"All work and no play will make Nina a very dull girl. Kyle still has that bottle of champagne." Topaz smiled at Nina.

"Dull is much safer, and leave Kyle out of this. So you definitely want to have this baby?"

"Of course I do. I know it's Germain's." She played with the charms dangling from the bracelet on her arm that Germain had given her at Disneyland.

"I believe it's Germain's baby, too." Nina blew smoke into the air. "But what if it's not? What if it's Sean's? Germain would never take you back and Jade would never take Sean back. That would be a disaster."

"I agree. That's why no one can ever know I'm pregnant."

"But you just said you were going to have the baby."

"I am. I can go another month or so without anyone knowing

I'm pregnant, and then you and I are going to leave the country until I have the baby."

"And go where and for how long? I have a life here and so do you." Nina looked like a crazy woman.

"I was thinking about Germany. Somewhere interesting with good hospitals outside the USA."

"How are we going to explain this to our friends? And don't forget you promised to perform at Keisha's fund-raiser in September."

"I won't be able to do that now. I've got more important things to do, you think?" She looked at Nina, who looked as bad as she felt.

"You're really serious about us leaving the country?"

"Yes." Topaz felt like screaming. She didn't feel like answering all of Nina's questions.

"And what about Turquoise? All you need is for her to tell Germain about Mommy's big stomach."

"You keep talking like the baby is Sean's when I know it's not."

"But what if it is Sean's? What are you going to do?"

Nina's dark eyes bore holes in her soul. Topaz gazed out at the grounds where the sprinklers shot water in long streams across the grass.

"I can't think about all that now." A frown clouded Topaz's pretty face. "You're the creative one. You'll think of something."

Chapter Twenty-eight

Nina sat in the window seat counting the droplets of rain clinging to the glass. She was bored. It was another cold, dreary day in London. She had read every book in the house and she wasn't in the mood for British television. So she stared at a string of cars held up in traffic. The bright red double-decker bus was the only splash of color in a background of muted gray.

London had been Nina's idea. They were able to remain in Los Angeles for the first four months of Topaz's pregnancy before the girls had to ship off to Europe. Nina left her job with MTV to work on Topaz's CD. Jamil, the producer, had gladly signed the confidentiality agreement, swearing him to secrecy, and accompanied them, thinking it would give him an opportunity to get back together with Nina.

But Nina had also chosen London because it was only a five-hour plane ride from New York City. She was still able to see Kyle, the one thing that brought her joy during all the madness, even though she had only been to see him once.

Topaz had left Turquoise with Germain and Chris. She couldn't have been happier when Germain gave her daughter the room next to Chris, and turned it into a pink castle for his little Barbie doll princess. She called them every night and talked for hours. Germain was too busy to take time off from his practice and it wasn't wise to let the children travel east when the weather was so cold, so she was able to keep her pregnancy a secret.

The telephone rang and Nina prayed it wasn't Jade. She had had a hard time talking to her ever since Topaz's confession. Neither of them had spoken to Keisha, who had to cancel the entire fundraiser after Topaz bailed out on her at the last minute.

Nina hung up the telephone and returned to the window seat. Helen, a certified midwife, was coming from the states to assist Topaz with the delivery. As long as there were no complications she would have the baby in the apartment.

"Hey, girl." Topaz waddled in laughing and singing and glowing like new money. Jamil followed her carrying two shopping bags with food.

"Ni-Ni, we bought Chinese food." She heard them in the kitchen getting plates and silverware. "Come on, Nina. I got your favorites. We got this from the restaurant in Piccadilly Circus."

"I'm not hungry." It amazed her that nothing ever seemed to bother her cousin. Nina thought she would be able to handle the situation, but all the lies and deception were beginning to take their toll. Things grew more difficult for her by the day. She had convinced herself that everything would be fine once the baby was born. She found her "Girlfriend" journal and began writing. It was her therapy.

"What's up, baby?" She heard smacking and smelled garlic. Jamil burped and shoveled another fork heaping with garlic chicken into his mouth. "Working on another one of your little stories?"

What did I ever see in you? I must have been drunk, high, and brain-damaged. She was just about to answer him when she heard a scream and the sound of breaking glass in the kitchen. They ran into the room and found Topaz holding on to the kitchen counter, the color drained from her face.

"I had a contraction." They helped her into the living room and onto the sofa. "Did Helen call?"

"She's flying as we speak. She'll be here in an hour. I thought the baby wasn't due until next week."

"Babies come when they get ready." Topaz laughed and sent Jamil into the kitchen for her food. "It's going to be a long night, people."

Before she could finish speaking, another contraction gripped her body. "Damn." Nina wiped her forehead with a cold washcloth. "It wasn't like this with my other babies."

Probably because you weren't trying to have the others in a foreign country without going to the hospital.

"Please don't have this baby before Helen gets here." Nina cut on the television for distraction while Jamil fanned Topaz.

"I'll try but my contractions are fifteen minutes apart." She pointed to a glass of ice and Jamil handed it to her.

"What does that mean?" Jamil looked worried.

"Your girl's about to have a baby . . . duh." Nina's patience was wearing thin.

"Maybe we should call 911 or get you to the hospital." Jamil picked up the phone.

"No," Nina and Topaz chorused.

"Someone's coming," Topaz added softly.

"Yeah, your baby, superstar. I'm calling the doctor."

"Jamil . . . no." Nina looked at Topaz. "No one can know about this baby, yet. Jamil, you have to swear you won't tell anyone."

"Your secret's safe with me. It'll follow me to my grave for a small price."

"What is it, Jamil? This isn't the time for you to play games."

"I'm not playing games." He looked at both of them and tried not to laugh. "All you have to do is get your girl to marry me."

Nina thought she would faint. "Are you serious?" Nina asked. Topaz looked in shock at Nina.

"Yes." Jamil folded his arms and looked at Nina.

"Nina, what do you have to say about it?"

Nina couldn't believe Topaz had the nerve to ask the question. "Hell no."

Nina was fuming. She knew Topaz would actually let her go through with it if it would keep her from losing Germain.

"I was just playing with y'all." Jamil laughed. "And I did sign that agreement."

"I was playing, too." Topaz laughed and then she nearly squeezed the life out of Jamil's hand.

The contractions were only minutes apart when Helen arrived. Nina was getting instructions from the hospital when Helen walked in the door.

"My God, girl. The baby's head is crowning. All you have to do is give me one good push."

Topaz pushed and minutes later the baby was out and crying.

"It's a girl . . . a beautiful baby girl." Helen washed the baby and Nina thought she would faint.

"Let me see her. I want to see her," Topaz demanded as she reached for the squirming bundle. Helen placed the infant in her arms and the smile quickly disappeared from her face. "Somebody take her." She lay back in the bed and faced the wall.

"I'll take her." Nina reached for the baby. She was a beautiful baby girl with cocoa skin and straight black hair, plastered to her tiny head.

"Is something wrong?" Helen looked at Nina and then at Topaz, who was crying, softly.

"She's just very tired. Why don't you give me a call tomorrow and we'll discuss names and the birth certificate then."

"Are you sure you don't want me to spend the night?"

"That won't be necessary. I'll give you a call if we need anything." Nina handed her an envelope and she left. She walked back into Topaz's room and sat on the bed.

"We have to get rid of her." Topaz was still facing the wall so she couldn't see Nina or the baby.

"Get rid of her? What do you mean get rid of her?" Nina placed the baby in the crib.

"Put her up for adoption. I can't keep her."

"Adoption? You can't do that. She's your baby."

"A baby by another woman's husband. Oh, my God. Why did she have to be Sean's? Why couldn't she be Germain's?"

"Only God knows."

"God is punishing me. Now get rid of that baby."

Nina could see Topaz was working herself up to a serious tantrum, so she took the crib and put the baby in her room and gave Topaz a Valium. Nina had just dozed off when the doorbell rang. She looked through the peephole and opened the door.

"Kyle? What are you doing here?" She had never been so glad to see anyone in her life.

"I'm not sure. Don't think I'm weird, but I am a preacher's kid and I learned two things from my parents . . . how to pray and how to hear from God." He looked at Nina and shook his head. "All day yesterday God kept telling me you needed me and to get over here, so I came as soon as I could. Is everything okay?"

Nina couldn't hold back the tears any longer. She fell into his arms and cried her eyes out.

"As usual, He was right. You do need me." He cuddled her like a baby and smoothed her hair, oblivious to the dark circles that had formed under her eyes and the pounds she had shed.

"I'm here now and I'll take care of you forever." He kissed away her tears.

The baby woke up crying and Nina rushed into the bedroom with a bottle.

"Whose baby is that, Nina?" Kyle watched as she picked her up and sat on the bed.

"It's a long story." Nina sighed.

"Here, let me." Kyle held the baby while she drank from the bottle. "She is so precious. It's amazing how they come here knowing how to do that."

When the baby finished eating she was out like a light. Kyle put her back in the crib bed and he lay next to Nina, listening intently while she told him everything.

"That's my niece? Oh, my God. She does look like my family, but she looks like she could be your daughter, too." Kyle got up and looked at the sleeping child. "And Topaz doesn't want her?"

"It's not that she doesn't want her. She just makes things very complicated."

"Complicated . . . I can't believe Sean. Kirk always said Topaz would be his worst nightmare. Was he ever right."

"Sean doesn't know anything about the baby. She doesn't want to ruin his marriage."

"It's kind of late for that. I wonder if she would be so concerned if Jade wasn't around."

"She and Sean were never more than friends. Neither one of them meant for anything to happen."

"What was my brother thinking?" Kyle shook his head.

"I don't think he was doing much thinking that night." Nina giggled. It was the first time she had laughed in months. Now that she had told Kyle everything, it felt as though the weight of the world had been lifted from her shoulders.

"He made it through the NBA without losing his virginity. I was surprised he did it, but I was very proud of him. He marries a wonderful woman and now this thing with Topaz . . . ugh. There's something I never told you. . . ."

"What is it?"

They whispered as they lay facing each other.

"I saw you that night at Jade's birthday . . . at the gallery opening."

"You did? Why didn't you say anything to me?"

"I was going to. I asked Sean who you were and when he told me you were Topaz's cousin, I said no way."

"No . . ." Nina fell back on the pillow, wanting to cry.

"And then our paths crossed again at the ranch. You were so beautiful I couldn't resist. And then I fell in love with you. . . ."

"You're in love with me?" Nina smiled into his eyes.

"Yes."

"Why?" She asked softly.

"Because of the way I feel when I'm around you."

"How do you feel?"

"Alive . . . like I can do anything."

"I feel like that, too."

They smiled at each other.

"You're sexy, sweet, and funny. You're one of the smartest women I've ever met and you're definitely the kindest. For some reason beautiful and kind don't usually go together."

"Really?"

"Really."

"When did you know you were in love with me?"

"You ask too many questions." He hopped up to look at the baby and then got under the covers and pulled her into his arms.

"It's cold." He jumped up and turned up the heat. "Gotta keep my girl warm. Both of them."

"It is cold and I can't wait to get back to LA. Now answer my question, Kyle."

"The day at the ranch."

"The day at the ranch what?" Nina propped her head up on her hands and looked him dead in the eye.

"I fell in love with you at the ranch when my dad called you up and you didn't hear him because of what I told you I'd do with that champagne. You should have seen your face." He fell back on the pillow and laughed until there were tears in his eyes.

"I was so embarrassed." She pulled the pillow from under him and hit him with it.

"Love taps . . . I know you love me." He laughed and she hit him harder.

"If you don't stop, I'm not going to give you what I have in my pocket."

"You are so nasty."

"You are too, you nasty girl. Now reach into my pocket. I bought you something."

"Sure you did." She looked skeptical as she reached into his pocket and put her hand on a ring box and pulled it out. "Kyle, what is this?"

"Open it and see."

She slowly opened the velvet case and gasped when she saw a platinum and diamond ring. "This is an engagement ring."

"No kidding? Woman, I told you I was here to take care of you forever. Now are you going to marry me so we can take our daughter home?"

"Our daughter? Kyle, I can't let you live a lie."

"You're not letting me do anything. That's my brother's child and we're going to raise her. I know you weren't going to let Topaz put her up for adoption. You're going to keep her, and raise her by yourself, aren't you?"

"Yes, but, Kyle, you don't have to marry me . . ."

"Nina, do you love me?"

She had never met a man so direct and straightforward. "Yes." All of a sudden she was nervous.

"Do you want to spend the rest of your life with me?"

Jade's words of wisdom hit her like a ton of bricks. She couldn't imagine her life without Kyle Ross.

Helen returned later that evening to fill in the rest of the information for the baby's birth certificate. It listed Kyle Ross and Nina Beaubien Ross as Kendall Nicole's parents.

Chapter Twenty-nine

Keisha took off her glasses and closed her books. She had been studying for a quiz in her grant writing class all morning. She had signed up for the class after Topaz and Nina had mysteriously disappeared to London. Something about their sudden departure still bothered Keisha, but Germain seemed fine with it.

She looked at the beautifully printed invitations for the benefit concert that had been wasted, but she couldn't blame Topaz for everything. She had thought the project would be so easy to do, but people in LA weren't as interested in the cause as they had been in Atlanta. She was amazed by their apathy, and without the others' assistance to solicit contributions, she had decided to pursue funding through government and private grants. She had wanted to set a new date in September, but she was still disappointed over the way everyone had dropped the concert like a hot potato. Everyone was so focused on themselves they didn't have time to think someone else could be in need.

She was so engrossed in her thoughts, she didn't realize Eric had come home and was standing over her.

"Whatcha doin'?" he whispered in her ear, and she jumped up to give him a hug. "Careful, baby, we've got company."

"Company?" She turned around and saw Sean standing behind her. "Sean." She hugged him and hoped she wouldn't cry. The twinkle was missing from his eyes and the sparkle from his smile. "Don't you ever disappear like that on us again."

"Go easy on him, baby. I already chewed him out." Eric went into the kitchen and Sean sat on the sofa next to Keisha.

"What's going on with you, Sean? Is everything all right?" Keisha watched Eric come back into the room with a King-sized Fatburger smothered with chili and cheese, french fries, and orange soda. "Look at you."

"Look at me." He rubbed his hands together and carefully unwrapped the burger. Keisha moved over next to him and smiled. "I thought you weren't going to eat any more junk food." He took a big bite of the burger and chewed it as though it was the best thing in the world.

"Man, you better give me a bite of that burger." He couldn't help laughing as he held the burger up to her lips for her to bite. She opened her mouth and he pulled the sandwich away before she could take a bite. "Eric, stop playing."

"Who's playing? Man, did you see how wide her mouth was open? She almost bit my hand off, not to mention my entire hamburger."

Keisha punched him several times, took the sandwich, and took several large bites while Sean laughed heartily. Eric went into the kitchen and brought out another hamburger and sat on the other side of the room away from Keisha.

"I always have a backup. She'll eat everything in sight when she's pregnant." Eric looked at Keisha and laughed while she started on his fries and drank the soda.

"You guys are expecting?" Sean was all smiles.

"In June. That's my son in the oven, right?" He looked at Keisha, who was finishing the last of the soda.

"I don't know why you're looking at me. I don't have anything to do with the sex of your children. You can have the rest of these fries, baby. I'm full."

"You guys are sick." Sean looked at Eric and laughed. "So Big Papa's got another one in the oven. Way to go, dog."

"I could use another man in the house to keep things in check around here. These women will eat and shop a brother out of house and home."

"Eric . . . I know Sean hasn't been here for so long that you have to show out. I'm going upstairs so you and your dog can bark alone."

"Wait, Keisha." Sean stood up and took her hand. "I need to talk to you and Eric."

"What's up, sweetie?" She sat down next to Eric and looked at Sean. He sat down and sighed.

"I guess you've been wondering what's been going on with me and Jade. Then I disappeared for a while. I've been trying to sort things out on my own. I need to talk to somebody and I'm too embarrassed to talk to my father."

"You don't have to be embarrassed about anything, man. We're all friends here. Getting married and staying married is no joke."

"I just don't know what happened. I watched my parents, Kirk and Karla, and then you and Keisha. You guys made it look so easy. I was the one always talking about getting married and we didn't even last a year."

"The first year is hard, Sean. Getting two people to become one is a process. It doesn't happen overnight. It takes a lot of compromising from both partners," Keisha explained. "You and Jade love each other. You'll work this out."

"We've been talking on the phone. I miss her and I miss Kobe. But I don't know if we can."

"Can what?" Eric demanded.

"Work things out," Sean finished softly.

"Why not? You still love her, right?"

"Yeah, but . . ."

"But what?" Eric was getting excited.

"Honey, calm down." Keisha took Eric by the hand. "Sean, Nina told me Jade didn't think you were attracted to her anymore. That's not true, is it?"

"Oh, my God, no." Sean put his head in his hands and started crying. "I never meant for it to happen."

Eric looked at Keisha, who moved beside him and held him.

"What happened, Sean?" She looked at Eric, who was practically climbing the wall.

"I'm attracted to my wife. I just couldn't make love to her after . . ." He stopped talking and sucked in his breath.

Keisha handed Sean a tissue. "After what?"

"I was with another woman." He spoke barely above a whisper.

"What do you mean you were with another woman?" Eric had a wild look on his face.

"Honey, let Sean tell us." Keisha met her husband's eye and gave him a look that said calm down.

"We made love."

"You had sex. Man, are you crazy?" There was no holding Eric back now.

"It didn't mean anything, but it's been killing me."

Eric opened his mouth and quickly closed it after Keisha gave him a dirty look.

"I haven't been able to face Jade."

Keisha handed him another tissue and silently prayed for God to give her something to say.

"Some of the greatest men of God have made the same mistake. The important thing is they asked God to forgive them. They fell down, but they got back up."

"Jade will never forgive me. I'm afraid my marriage is over."

"Was this someone you were seeing? I don't understand how this happened." Eric was finally calm enough to speak.

"It just happened. I should never have had that champagne."

"Champagne? I've never seen you take a drink in my life," Eric said.

"That's why I don't drink. I get a drop of alcohol in my system and I act a fool. You would think I'd learned that lesson in college. Jade was out of town. If I could have gone home and made love to my wife, maybe I wouldn't have ended up in someone else's bed."

"Dang, man. Do you think this would have happened if Jade hadn't cut off the action in the bedroom?"

"I'm sure that played a small part, but I should have been able to control myself. But the hardest thing I've had to deal with is that I enjoyed it."

"Don't beat yourself up, it was just sex, pure unadulterated lust. Right? You're not in love with this woman?"

"Oh, hell no." Sean covered his mouth. "I'm sorry."

Eric looked at Keisha. "You're just being honest, Sean. It took a lot of courage for you to tell us this. But, I think you've allowed the enemy to magnify the situation in your mind long enough. He wanted you to think what you did with this other woman was better, because he wants to destroy your marriage."

"You're right. I should have spoken to you about this long ago."

"Yeah, man, you need to be with your wife. Too much time has gone by already." Eric was calm again.

"You guys need to do a whole lot of talking and you definitely need to see a counselor. As far as your one-night stand, that's between you and God," Keisha finished.

Eric took the dirty dishes into the kitchen and brought Keisha a bowl of strawberry ice cream.

"How did you know I wanted this?" She smiled up at him.

"I know you." He opened his mouth and she gave him a spoonful of ice cream.

"All I ever wanted is a relationship like you guys and I made a mess." Sean watched them eating her ice cream.

"Man, you can have a relationship like this, but someone has to be willing to sacrifice. It takes work. Relationships don't just happen. Keisha's been here for me every step of the way. There's nothing I wouldn't do for her. My grandmother always told me to give a woman what I wanted to receive from a woman."

"I thought that's what I was doing. . . ." Sean jumped up and started toward the door. "I want my marriage and I'll do whatever it takes."

Eric flopped down on the sofa next to Keisha. "Can you believe that? I never thought Sean, of all people, would have an affair."

"Why are you so surprised?" She flipped on the television.

"Aren't you?" Eric was still in shock.

"Not really."

"Why?"

"Because he's human and people make mistakes and I know his wife."

"Keisha."

"I know, baby. I was just playing." She laughed. "I think those two have a chance at something special if they're willing to forgive and forget."

"That's the key, if they're willing to forgive and forget. I wonder what hoochie got a hold of him. You don't know how badly I wanted to ask."

"I know. . . ." Keisha giggled and Eric laughed out loud.

She picked up a pillow and smacked him with it. "It's not that funny. If you ever did that to me I'd cut it off."

"Dang, girl, why are you women always threatening to cut a brother's stuff off? That's cold-blooded."

"Probably because you brothers have a tendency to put it where it doesn't belong."

"Well, you'll never have to worry about me doing anything like that. I'm a good dog. Think we can get a quickie before Kendra gets home? All this talk about sex made me want some." He pretended to pant like a puppy.

"Like you don't always want some."

They were just about to go upstairs when the telephone rang. Keisha sat down on the couch in slow motion as she listened.

"You're kidding? I don't believe it."

"What happened? Who did it?" Eric whispered loudly as he watched her expressions.

"That was Topaz and you'll never believe who got married."

"Who? Topaz?"

"No . . . Nina."

"Nina? Baby girl got married? Who was the lucky guy? Jamil?"

"No. Kyle."

"Kyle? What?" Eric jumped up and looked like a wild man. "Get outta here. My dog? Mr. I'll Never Get Married?"

Keisha nodded her head. "But guess what else?"

"There's more?"

"Yes. You better sit down for this one."

"What?" He promptly sat down.

"They have a baby, a little girl. Kendall Nicole."

Eric opened his mouth and closed it. "Ooh . . ."

"Folks have seriously been creepin' and sleepin' up in here." They both laughed till they were in tears.

"And those Ross brothers are just full of surprises."

Chapter Thirty

Jade carefully spread sticky rice over seafood and covered that with a mixture of shrimp and avocado for her own special brand of California rolls. She had also prepared fried plantain, Japanese salad and soup, and several types of pan-fried dumplings. There was also baked chicken with jerk sauce and potato salad. She remembered what it was like to be pregnant and hungry so she wanted to be sure Keisha was fed well. She was making lunch especially for her.

Jade had been lonely ever since Nina had run off to London with Topaz. Sean was still keeping his distance, and painting wasn't as much fun as it used to be. Akiba and Kiyoko ran the gallery. She had a showing in June to celebrate her second year in business, but that was the only thing scheduled. She had plenty of free time now, but no husband. It was closing the barn door after the horse had run away. She missed her husband. She had been selfish and she had taken him for granted.

She couldn't believe Kobe was almost a year old. She picked up her son and kissed him. It was amazing how much he looked like Sean except for the eyes. The concierge phoned as she was brushing his hair.

"Your godmother is here, Kobe. Let's go meet her." She opened the door just as Keisha rang the bell. "Look, Kobe, look who's here."

Keisha took the little boy from Jade and kissed him. "I can't believe this is my first time at your apartment. This is really nice."

"Oh, my God. I can't believe I never had you over. I'm sorry. I don't know who that crazy woman was. I always felt so insecure because you were just the consummate housewife and mother." She led Keisha into the kitchen and prepared their plates.

"You shouldn't feel like that. You're good at so many things. You're smart and you're beautiful. You're a fabulous painter. You're a wife and a mother. I was feeling so insecure when we first moved here. I wanted something else to do and you were always telling me I needed to get a life, and you don't know how badly I felt I needed one." Keisha laughed.

"I was so horrible. I'm sorry. I should never have said that." Jade wiped a tear from her eye.

"And then I started tripping about how I looked. People told me how bad LA is for relationships and I was concerned about my marriage." Keisha used chopsticks to dip a dumpling in hot oil.

"Not you, Keisha. You should see how Eric looks at you. He adores you. And you're gorgeous. I always loved your braids. I wish I could do something else with mine." She ran her fingers through her long straight hair.

"I remember when I first saw you. I told Eric Sean had found himself a black Barbie doll."

"Me?" Jade laughed. "I never thought I was pretty."

"Why not?" Keisha was surprised.

"I never fit in. I was always so different. There was never anyone for me to identify with."

"But that's the wonderful thing about black women. I think we are the most beautiful women on the planet. We look all kinds of ways and we come in all colors, sizes, and shapes."

"I wish I'd had friends like you, Nina, and Topaz when I was little. Maybe I wouldn't have been so crazy. I never realized how important it is to have girlfriends until I met all of you. That day when we were having lunch and Topaz came in and started talking, I had never done that before. Now she's gorgeous. I was so jealous of her. I know Sean used to like her. But that's in the past now."

"Topaz is very pretty. We've been best friends since kindergarten. Most people never get to know her to see how much fun she is. She's getting married in June. There's a lot going on that month."

"Are you still doing the fund-raiser in September?"

"I don't know."

"I'll be glad to do the poster and I'll ask Sean about the ranch." Jade cleared the away the dishes and took out a cheesecake. "From the Factory." She smiled. "Remember you're eating for two."

Keisha took a bite and moaned. "This is so good. You look real good, Jade. Have you been working out?"

"Yes, you can tell?" Jade looked down at herself as she placed a sliver of cake on her plate.

"Yes, girl. You look wonderful."

"Thanks, my mother was hounding me. I've been down in the exercise room every day and I even got my navel pierced." She lifted her top and showed Keisha the green stone dangling from her belly button.

"You and Nina. That's too much pain for me."

"It didn't really hurt." Jade looked down at the ring in her navel.

"Lunch was so good, Jade. You should open a restaurant with Jamaican and Japanese cuisine. People would love it. Celebrity-owned restaurants are always real popular."

"You think? It might be a nice project for Sean and me to do together. . . ." She looked at Keisha to see what she would say.

"It might. But you and Sean need to spend time talking and rekindling your relationship before you try to open a restaurant."

"You're right. Somewhere things got off track. I thought once we were married, things would just fall into place. I guess I was pretty naive. Both of my parents always worked. I thought Sean and I would be like them."

"Your mother wasn't married to one of the biggest stars in the NBA. You guys had a lot to deal with and then you became pregnant."

"Nina told me how you helped Topaz. Do you think you can help me and Sean get back together?"

Jade was another person. Keisha couldn't remember when she had seen her so humble. This was the woman she had met in the Bahamas.

"You and Eric have such a great relationship," Jade continued. "What's your secret?"

Keisha laughed at the thought. "Oh, there are days when I could kill him, but we always make time for each other. We talk a lot and we laugh at everything. He's a very good listener. He's my best friend. I prayed and asked God to teach me how to love him and to teach Eric how to love me."

"That's so special," Jade whispered, teary eyed.

"If he does something that bothers me, I don't nag him, I tell God and God knows how to talk to him."

"You are so smart. How did you learn all of this?"

"I don't always feel so smart. I went to a lot of women's Bible studies."

"I want to go with you to the next class."

"Good. It'll help you learn to balance all those things you're so good at. The spiritual part of marriage is having God in the center."

"I never thought about it that way. Sean and I used to pray together and then I got so busy, I never had time for anything. But I still should have prayed for us and about the things that were bothering me instead of getting mad at him all the time."

"I make Eric feel like he's the most important person in the world. He's very good to me. He treats me like a queen, and he's my king."

"I see so many things I did wrong now. Hindsight is twenty-

twenty. Once I got pregnant, I never felt like making love. I should have explained that to Sean instead of just pushing him away." Sadness clouded her pretty face.

"You can't focus on what you didn't do, you need to focus on what you're going to do to get him back."

"He's up at the ranch. I was thinking about going up there to see him. What do you think?" She looked at Keisha hopefully.

"I think you should do what's in your heart. He's your husband. Go jump that fine man's bones. Show off that cute little navel ring. You are a woman and he's a man. Some things always work."

"I feel so unsure, almost like my first time with him."

"My first time with Sean was very special. I'll always remember my wedding night."

"I'm sure." Keisha made a face and Jade laughed.

"You are so funny." She sat there smiling at Keisha.

"Why are you still sitting here?" Keisha crossed her arms and looked at Jade as if she were crazy.

"What?"

"It's nice outside. Go put on one of those hoochie mama tops that you and Nina bought when you got your navel pierced . . ."

"Did she tell you?"

"No, but I know Nina. Put on some tight jeans, your makeup . . . you know how to work those almond eyes, and take a little drive. And don't forget that sexy nightgown Topaz gave you. Now I'm taking my godson to my house. Eric's out of town. I can use some company."

Jade jumped into her convertible and headed up the coast.

I've got to do this while I've still got the nerve.

She pulled into the driveway and felt her stomach do flip-flops when she saw his Range Rover parked by the side of the house. She found him sitting on the deck reading a book.

She straightened her top and walked out on the deck. "Nice day, huh." She smiled at him as she bent over, stretched her body over the railing on the deck.

Sean closed his book and sat up and paid attention. "Jade . . ."

She walked straight to him and put her arms around him. "I've missed you so much, baby. I'm so sorry for everything." She kissed him before he had a chance to say anything.

"I'm sorry, too." He kissed her and held her tightly. "I was starting to think I'd never hold you in my arms again."

"I'll always be here for you to hold. Now you don't go anywhere. I'll be right back."

She returned with a CD player and turned it on and started to dance. She stood in front of him and did a very sensual belly dance.

"I'll be your private dancer."

"Come here, baby."

He called me baby. She smiled and danced her way over to him.

Those dance lessons really came in handy. Keisha was right. I am a woman and I'll be the only hoochie he ever knows about. I'll make sure of that.

Chapter Thirty-one

Topaz could barely stand still as she watched Germain sign his name on their marriage license in Las Vegas. Turquoise sat on the counter watching him write. "Want pen, Daddy."

He picked her up and kissed her before he handed the gold pen to Topaz. "Mommy has to use it first, Baby Doll."

She took the pen and drew her pouty lips together in a kiss and quickly scribbled *Topaz Black*. They were actually getting married tonight. The day she had dreamed of had finally arrived.

"Daddy and I named Turquoise Baby Doll. We never call her Turquoise anymore." Chris was such a little man and extremely intelligent.

Topaz covered her mouth to keep from laughing. "Baby Doll? I heard you guys calling her that. I'm sure Baby Doll was running the house while I was away, too." Topaz looked at her daughter and smiled. Gunther only provided the seed; she was the spitting image of Topaz in golden bronze. The family had come directly from the airport to the license bureau. They would be married at midnight at the Venetian.

Germain and Chris walked out to the limo chatting excitedly

about the roller coasters they were going to ride while Topaz and the ladies had a girlfriend afternoon at the spa.

When they arrived at the hotel Jade, Sean, Kyle, and Nina were getting out of another limo.

"Hey, Topaz, congratulations. Your dream finally came true." Jade gave her a quick peck on the cheek.

"Thanks, Jade. You are looking wonderful." Topaz's words were sincere as she admired Jade. She was too cute with her hair in a ponytail with a gorgeous green silk outfit that exposed her navel jewelry tastefully.

"I got my man back." She grinned as Sean turned to face Topaz. Their eyes met for the first time since the night he left her bed.

That is one fine man and he is an incredible lover. I am so glad you got your act together, Jade. If I didn't love my husband and if you weren't my friend . . .

"Hello, Topaz." Sean gave her a quick peck on the cheek. "I'm glad to see the brother got his head on straight." He spoke so only she could hear. "You look happy, too."

She smiled, relieved that he showed no telltale signs of their brief interlude. She kissed Nina and looked away quickly when she saw the nanny with Nicki and Kobe.

Brother and sister . . . together . . . this is crazy. Sean may have been able to push that night out of his mind, but every time she looked at Nicki she remembered.

Nina gave her a warning glance as she spotted Germain and Kyle laughing and talking like long lost friends.

Another fine brother and this one has Nina climbing the bedroom walls. There's something to be said about the sons of a preacher man.

"Congratulations, Topaz." He kissed her on the cheek and walked away. Kyle never said much and she knew he didn't like her. She always felt as though he was looking down at her. Nina had said she was paranoid, but there was always a slight chill in the air whenever he came around.

"I didn't know you knew Nina's husband." Topaz focused her amber eyes on her soon to be husband.

"Kyle is my boy. He's a nut. I met him when Keisha was in Jersey. We hit it off immediately and we always get together whenever one of us is in the other's city."

Good old Keisha. She just knows everybody. She's the one who linked us all together.

"Where is my matron of honor? I hope she didn't have the baby yet."

"Nope . . . there she is." Germain started laughing and so did everyone else when they spotted her waddling up to the entrance of the hotel with Eric and Kendra.

"We know what y'all been doin'." Germain kissed Keisha and she poked him.

"Yeah and we all know what y'all gettin' ready to do."

"Get him, girl." Topaz laughed as she attempted to hug Keisha and her belly.

"Damn, girl. How do you and Eric be workin' this?"

"The same way you and Germain did."

It was a noisy group that checked into suites on the penthouse floor.

"Okay, Germain, you have to leave and take your children with you." Topaz smiled as she kissed them all, lingering over Germain. "I'll see you later, handsome, for our date at midnight." He grinned and she patted him on the behind as she closed the door. "Have fun, you guys."

Keisha knocked on the door before she could open a suitcase to unpack. "I'm hungry, girl. Let's go down to the spa so we can eat. Don't forget Nina's shower gift. I still can't get over her and Kyle eloping."

"I didn't know either and I was in the same apartment with her. She took out a Victoria's Secret shopping bag. "I got Miss Hot to Trot a *Kama Sutra* kit."

"Like she really needs it. That Nicole is so precious."

"She is. Now let's go so we can check out the Shoppes. I saw the cutest little black dress that will drive Germain crazy."

Nina and Jade were having massages and sipping Cristal when they arrived. They got undressed and joined the others on the massage tables.

"It's girlfriend day," Topaz sang after she was handed a glass of champagne.

"Let's get something to eat." Keisha, who had to sit up for her back massage, was looking at a menu. The others laughed themselves to tears as they teased the very expectant mother.

"Nina, how did you get so skinny so fast, and you barely showed? I hate skinny people like you." Keisha made a face at Nina and studied the lobster salad sitting in front of her.

"Yeah, how did you get so skinny so fast? You didn't even gain an ounce of fat." Jade poked her on the thigh and the taut, firm flesh barely moved.

"And she still has those perky little tits. I bet Kyle has a field day with those things." Topaz laughed and the others joined in.

"Hate the game, not the player." Nina was ever so cool as she sipped a Long Island iced tea.

"Y'all gettin' nasty up in here." Keisha was trying to keep a straight face. And I'm hating the player." She stared at Nina's chest and then her own.

"That's okay, boo. My husband, Dr. Gradney, you know, the world-famous cosmetic surgeon? He can hook those girls up." Topaz gave Keisha a wicked grin as Keisha's mouth dropped open in shock. "Wait, I don't know if I want Germain working on your boobs," Topaz added.

"You are so nasty." Keisha hit Topaz with her linen napkin. "I don't want Germain doing anything with my boobs. I happen to like them the way they are and so does Eric."

"You guys are so funny." Jade dabbed at the corner of her eye with her napkin.

"Don't think you're exempt from this conversation, Mrs. Jade Ross. I won't even start on what Sean does with his tongue and that navel ring. Nina told me what Kyle does and Sean is his brother." Topaz smiled at the sister-in-laws as Nina spat out her last sip of iced tea.

"Stop, before I have this baby right here. Somebody gag her." Keisha wiped her forehead with a towel. She had broken into a sweat.

"Oh, no." Jade laughed.

"She has an audience. You know how she likes to perform." Nina pulled Topaz into a headlock and gently thumped her forehead. "Take this shower gift before I beat you with it. Congratulations, cuz. I hope you and the doc will be very happy." She kissed her and handed her a beautifully wrapped gift.

"Congratulations." Keisha and Jade produced gifts, too.

"Aw, you guys, this is so special. This is my third marriage and my first bridal shower." Topaz looked like a kid on Christmas Day as she tore paper off a box.

"That's because she never had any girlfriends." Keisha laughed. "They all hated her because their boyfriends thought she was fine." Keisha placed a large bow from one of the packages on her head.

"Don't hate the player, hate the game, darling, hate the game."

All the ladies pooh-poohed Topaz and pulled out another set of boxes.

"Ms. Perky." Keisha looked at Nina and tried to keep a straight face. "We couldn't forget you. Even though we weren't invited to the wedding, congratulations."

They opened all their gifts and posed for pictures and then went over to the beauty parlor and had their nails, toes, and makeup done. Germain's nanny brought Turquoise down so she could have her hair done, too.

"Want nail polish, Mommy." Topaz agreed and everyone in the

salon made a fuss over her while she sat there ever so patiently for the manicurist to apply the pearl-white polish.

"You know Germain and Chris gave her a new name. This is Baby Doll."

"She is a little doll. But you better not let them spoil her. She'll be just like you." Keisha laughed.

Nina helped Topaz into the sexy white silk sheath that flowed over her skin like melted butter.

"Now where's the dress?" Nina looked around the room. "Because I know this is only the slip."

"You know this is the dress. You were with me when I bought it in London." Topaz looked at the dress in the mirror.

"You were serious? I thought you were playing. You can't wear any underwear with that." Nina put her hands on her hips.

"I knew these would come in handy. Here's your something blue." Jade blushed and handed Topaz a gift bag from one of the boutiques downstairs.

Topaz reached inside and pulled out a midnight-blue satin thong. "I am so glad all of you are married women with fine, wonderful husbands or else y'all would really be hating tonight." She did a sexy little dance.

"That thong, thong, thong, thong," Nina sang and everyone was laughing again.

"That's what Sisqo was talking about in that song? I thought he was singing about a flip-flop."

"A flip-flop?" Topaz looked at her as if she were crazy.

"You know those things you wear to the beach? Thongs." Keisha pulled Kendra's braids into a ponytail while the others laughed.

"Keisha, you're ruining everyone's makeup. Let's go downstairs."

They freshened their makeup and tried not to laugh.

The ladies arrived in two gondolas, steered through the canal to the piazza, where the men were waiting. Nicki and Kobe were upstairs asleep under the watchful eye of their nannies.

Topaz joined Germain under the bridge, where they recited

vows to each other. She handed Keisha her flowers and Germain took her hands in his.

"I pledge my love to you for all eternity. You are my beautiful queen, the mother of my children, my soul mate, my life. I love you, baby, with all my heart and this time it's gonna last forever." He kissed her and everyone smiled.

Topaz was breathless from his kiss. "Dang, baby."

Nina howled with laughter. Then she whispered in Keisha's ear, "She is blasted. I know she's been drinking Cristal all day. You know how girlfriend loves her champagne."

Keisha smiled and looked at her friend, who was reciting her vows to Germain.

"You are my beautiful king, my African warrior. My babies' daddy, and my partner in every way for life. I adore you. You are the most wonderful man and I am eternally grateful to God to have you back in my life." She broke into tears and he pulled her into his arms and held her.

"I'm okay. I'm just happy. I love this man, y'all." She kissed him and every one cat-whistled.

"Drama," Nina whispered to Keisha. "She's always on stage."

They exchanged platinum bands inscribed with their names and the date, and the minister pronounced them husband and wife. Everyone posed for countless photos. The beautiful candlelit ceremony had been videotaped as well.

Topaz and Germain stood under the piazza and kissed again for the photographers. "Rumor has it, Dr. Gradney, that whoever kisses under this bridge is destined to be together forever."

"Oh yeah?" He kissed her until she was breathless. If there was anything Germain could do, it was kiss. Out of all the men she had ever been with, he was the best, at everything.

They sat down to dinner with champagne and cake at Emeril Lagasse's restaurant in the hotel. Afterward, they went dancing. Germain pulled Topaz into his arms.

"My baby ain't wearing no drawers." He grabbed her butt and

she screamed softly. "Look at you, girl. You want some bad. We're going upstairs so I can give you what you need, Mrs. Gradney."

Sean and Jade walked up as they were on their way out of the club. Topaz looked at Sean while the couples exchanged greetings and imagined his lips, brushing against hers ever so gently.

Chapter Thirty-two

Nina handed a stack of Federal Express envelopes to one of the younger security guards on the property. He lit up like a Christmas tree the moment he laid eyes on her. "It's so good to have you back, Miss Nina."

"How's the music?"

"Tight. I'll have that tape ready for Jamil next week."

"Cool. Let me know."

She closed the door and smiled at Kyle, who was on the Internet trading stocks. He held a pencil between his lips as he typed on the keys.

"I heard you flirting with the security guard." He had removed the pencil from his lips and put it back.

"I was not flirting, I'm just excited about my manuscripts. I can't believe my novel is finished." She pulled the pencil out of his lips and kissed him.

"I just deleted all my Microsoft stock. I told you about doing that while I'm trying to work."

"You are so sick." She laughed and kissed him again. He clicked off the computer and grabbed her.

"And you are too sweet. . . . So which publishing house shall I buy stock in?" He pulled her hair out of the ponytail and kissed her gently on the stomach.

"Simon and Schuster. Kyle, we have to meet the Realtor in half an hour to get the keys to the house." She laughed when he unzipped her pants.

"That's all we need."

They had chosen a house in the Malibu Colony. Nina had warned them things would get crazy when the rainy season hit, but they had both fallen in love with the waterfront estate.

Nina had almost choked when Kyle informed the agent that a loan would not be necessary and he would be making the purchase for the entire amount with a cashier's check.

The five-bedroom house had been in foreclosure. It was brand-new. The builder fell on hard times and had to unload it quick and they bought the home at a small percentage above cost. The builder had overspent on the amenities and the house was a palace.

The peg and groove hardwood floors were the color of caramel. The bathrooms and kitchen were Italian marble. There were high cathedral ceilings in every room of the split-level first floor and wonderful fireplaces. In their bedroom they loved the fireplace that could also be enjoyed from the bathtub. The house was flashy and gorgeous just like them, and a definite investment.

"Now you can look at the water while you write. My baby's a big-time author." They were standing in the room that would be her office looking at the waves as they crashed over boulders on the beach. It was also close to Nicki's suite on the second floor.

"I don't know about all that. Someone still has to buy it."

"Baby, it's like R. Kelly sang. If I believe it, then I can see it."

"I know. You're right. I'm so glad God gave me you."

"I never prayed for a wife . . . Well, I did when I was little. We all did. Kirk found his early. It took Sean and me a little longer. I know my daddy didn't think I would get married, but I was waiting for what I asked for."

"And what was that?" Nina smiled into his eyes as their fingers intertwined.

"Someone sweet and sexy, smart and beautiful, with a sense of humor." He smiled back into her eyes. "I guess I had to wait so long because you were a baby. I had to wait for you to grow up. I laugh every time I think about, that when you were ten, I was sixteen."

"That is funny." Nina laughed. "Dang, Kyle, you are an old man. And I didn't like boys when I was ten."

"You would have liked me. I was so fresh then. If Kenny Ross knew about the trouble I used to get Kirk into with me, he would have killed me."

"I don't even want to know. I can only imagine."

"You don't have to. When I saw you I said Kyle has to get some of that." He kissed her and she pulled away.

"You just thought you were all that and a bag of chips."

"I am." He laughed. "But the only woman I want to corrupt now is you, but you've done a pretty good job of corrupting me. Delilah's cousin is so delightful."

"You are so bad. How did Sean end up being a virgin with you as a brother?"

"He was always somewhere playing basketball. If he had hung with me he wouldn't have any outside babies. He should have hit that long ago and got her out of his system."

"Topaz always complained because he wouldn't give up the booty. I'm glad she loves her husband. He should never have been the one to bring her home that night. She hadn't been with anyone since her husband died. And Miss T loves to get her swerve on."

"Well, she's married now and Sean and Jade are back together and none of them will ever know."

"Did you tell Kirk? Jade told me the two of you are extremely close."

"We are. He's been my best friend forever. But this is our secret, just between us."

"And Topaz," Nina added.

"I'm not worried about her. She loves Germain. I've been convinced ever since the wedding. She won't open her mouth."

"And Nicki doesn't exist in her world."

When they arrived back at the house in Bel Air, Rosa met them at the door with Nicole, crying in her arms.

"She's been fussy all day, Miss Nina. I don't think she feels well."

Nina took the baby and cuddled her to her breast.

"She won't eat either."

"What's wrong with Mama's pretty baby?" She sang and cooed to the baby, who stopped crying and smiled. Nina her some milk and she drew on the nipple for seconds and started to cry again.

"You try, baby." She handed him the baby and the bottle.

"Nicki, baby, drink some milk for Daddy." She screamed even louder and Kyle looked at Nina.

"I'm calling the pediatrician." She dashed to the phone while Kyle sent Rosa upstairs for her bag.

"Dr. Felder said to bring her in."

The sound of Nina's cell phone ringing was clearly audible as they drove to Cedars in silence.

"Our dinner reservations are for eight. I'm telling you now so you and Kyle have plenty of time to get ready so you don't walk in for dessert." Nina was glad to hear Jade so happy and laughing again.

"We won't be able to make it. We're on the way to the hospital with Nicki."

"What's wrong?"

"We just got back from Malibu, and Rosa said she'd been fussy all day. She has a little fever, too."

"She's too young to be cutting teeth," Jade reasoned. "We'll meet you over there."

"You don't have to . . ." Nina never finished her sentence because Jade had hung up.

"Jade and your brother are coming to the hospital."

"I don't know what for, I'm sure it's only a summer cold."

By the time they were seen in the ER, Nicole's fever was over a hundred. Nina could barely watch as the nurse drew several tubes of blood from her for tests. The nurse informed them Jade and Sean were in the waiting room, so Kyle went out and Jade came in.

"What's wrong with her?" Jade rubbed Nicki's little hand between her fingers.

"They don't know. They're running tests."

"Your daughter has sickle cell disease," the doctor informed Nina.

"She has what?"

"Sickle cell disease. It's a disease of the red blood cells found primarily in African-Americans." The doctor paused while the in-laws searched one another's faces.

"That's what Keisha wanted to raise money for." Jade remembered. "Her father is a specialist. She'll know what to do."

Jade dialed on her cell while Nina racked her brain trying to remember the things Keisha had said. Those meetings seemed like eons ago. So many things had happened since then.

"She's on her way." Jade put an arm around Nina's shoulder. "Everything will be okay."

My baby has sickle cell disease.

"Doctor, how did this happen?" She could barely speak. Kyle sat down beside her and took her hand.

"It takes two parents with the trait to produce the disease. You should have been made aware of that when you were married."

"We were married in Europe." Nina could feel Kyle's pulse beating in his hand.

"But you should have been notified by the health department

within a couple weeks after your daughter's birth." The doctor flipped through the chart and wrote some orders.

"My daughter was born in Europe, too. Will she be all right?"

"She has a little swelling here in her fingers. That's why I decided to test for sickle cell. She's probably a little uncomfortable from the sickling; that's when her red blood cells change their shape. I'm going to give her an IV and some Tylenol and see how she does before I decide if we need to admit her to the hospital."

"Sean has the trait. It was in the paperwork the accountant put together for the life insurance policy," Jade informed them. Nina looked at Kyle, who hadn't let go of her hand once. She looked up and saw Eric and Keisha standing outside the door.

They walked in and greeted everyone and Keisha talked to Nina and Kyle.

"You both have the trait, but Nicki's going to be just fine. That's why it's so important for people to be tested." Keisha's tone was warm and very reassuring.

Topaz has the trait. I wonder if Kyle has it, too.

"Kyle, did you pray for Nicki?" Keisha stroked his hand.

"I was so upset, I forgot. I'm still getting used to this daddy thing. You lead the prayer for us, Key."

She nodded and the group drew into a small circle and held hands while she laid hands on the baby and declared her healed. Nicki was sleeping peacefully when Topaz burst into the room in tears.

"Oh, my God, what's wrong with my baby? She's not going to die, is she?"

Nina jumped up and led Topaz out of the room. "What is wrong with you? Do you want to blow this thing sky-high?" She walked Topaz down the hall, whispering through gritted teeth.

"God's punishing me, isn't he? I slept with Sean and now my baby's going to die." She fumbled in her purse for a tissue.

Nina grabbed her by the arm and held her tightly. "Would you get a quick grip? She is not going to die." She looked at Topaz and shook her head. "I thought we settled this in London."

"That was before she got sick." Tears streamed out of her eyes. "She's still my daughter, Nina, and I want her to have the best medical care."

"Let's get one thing straight, right here, right now, for once and forever. She is not *your daughter*. You didn't want her, remember? She belongs to me and Kyle now. We're her parents and we'll make sure she has whatever she needs."

Chapter Thirty-three

Keisha sat down in the nursery to feed her newly born son. Somehow, she had survived the hilarity of the wedding in Vegas, and Eric Johnson Jr. was born in Los Angeles. He was born the same night they returned. She focused on Rick, who had a healthy set of lungs, with his little mouth stretched wide open.

"You are just like your daddy, boy." The moment he got the first drop of milk, he was silent.

"What is she doing to you, man?" Eric walked into the room and knelt down behind her to look at his son.

"He's just acting like his daddy. I want it and I want it now." Keisha spoke like Eric and he grinned.

"I don't act like that when I'm hungry." He looked at her innocently.

"Who said I was talking about food?" She gave him a look and he doubled over laughing.

"We won't talk about what you do to make me act like that."

"No, we won't. Not for another month."

"A whole month?" The telephone rang and he went to answer it. "It's Nina. I'll put him down." He took the baby and handed her the phone. "Saved by the bell."

"Keisha, what's up with the fund-raiser? Can we do it this September?"

"Are you talking about A Chocolate Affair?" Keisha hadn't looked at her file since class ended. Things had gotten crazy with Kendra finishing first grade and the Lakers in the playoffs. Then there was the wedding and Rick's birth.

"I haven't thought about the concert in months."

"But can we do it?"

"You're serious, aren't you?"

"I spoke to Topaz. She's going to sing. They just dropped her first single. Jamil's label is sponsoring the tab for food and drinks. Jade designed the poster. She did it about a month ago. It's tight. I can drop the artwork at Kinko's. I just need a date from you."

"And you asked me if we could do it? You've done it, girl. How's my baby, girl?"

"Wonderful and healed. Things become a little more important when they affect you. I remember you being so angry when you realized people didn't seem to care. We care and we're going to do something about it."

"Let's do it, girl." Keisha was excited.

"I'll drive in so we can go over everything."

"Hey, when am I going to see this chocolate star pad you and Kyle bought in Malibu?"

"It's not ready yet. We're gonna have all you guys over for a party soon."

"Jade said it's something else. She mentioned waterfalls and lights."

"She only saw it from the outside." Nina laughed. "She and Sean drove over here one night, uninvited, and they thought we were going to let them in. We took them out to dinner and then they got mad at us when they realized we were serious and drove to the ranch."

"You two are awful. Just like two little bad kids. I'll see you later."

She patted Rick, who was sleeping soundly, and found her husband in the family room camped out on the sofa.

"My baby's tired." She stroked him on the cheek and sat down on the other sofa. "Can I get you anything?"

"No, baby. Thanks." He stretched his body and moaned. "You can always give a brother a massage with those magic fingers of yours."

"I'll get the Ben Gay. You need a valve and lube job after eighty-two games." She massaged the ointment into his back with her fingers and he moaned.

"That's not all I need, baby. So what was Miss Nina talking about? Sean told me that she and Kyle wouldn't let them in the house. He was really hot. See what happens to a good brother when one of you gets her hooks in him?"

"If she's a friend of mine, he'll be a better brother." She smiled as she kneaded his shoulder.

"I wonder how the doctor and his bride are doing. She is such a drama queen. She was as high as a kite at that wedding."

"They're on their honeymoon. And she was happy, but she did drink a lot of champagne."

"Champagne?" He almost fell off the couch laughing. "That would be something if she was the hoochie who got a hold of Sean."

"Topaz wouldn't do a thing like that. And she's not a hoochie." Keisha's fingers burned from the ointment and her mind was racing.

"That's your girl, you would know, but I'll never stop saying that superstar has her own agenda . . . herself. What was that scene at the hospital all about?"

"That was a bit strange." She wiped Eric's back with a towel. "She was more upset than Nina."

"Yeah," Eric agreed. "The way she carried on, you would have thought it was her child."

The doorbell rang before either one of them had a chance to say another word. Eric went to answer it and returned with Nina. She

A CHOCOLATE AFFAIR

gave Keisha a hug and proceeded to take folders out of her brief-case.

"Baby, I almost forgot. We're having the concert, our Chocolate Affair."

"You're kidding!" An easy smile covered his handsome face.

"I already spoke to some of your boys. We need Shaq and Kobe Bryant to come." Nina made some notes on a pad.

"Cool. I'll give them a call."

"Kyle got American Express to buy a bunch of thousand-dollar seats. So we have some free tickets. Stars always want everything for free, but I'm going to make everyone buy a ticket."

"I'm sure you will." Eric laughed. "I'm going to start working on the celebrity basketball game."

"Sean's putting together a team. He said you're gonna get stomped. He wants to get some of his retired buddies like Magic and Barkley to play."

"Oh, it's like that now?" Eric howled with laughter. "He was sup-posed to be playing with me. We'll clean up the floor with those old boys."

Keisha and Nina looked at each other and grinned as they went over the details of the day.

"I never thought it would happen. I can't wait to tell Daddy."

"It was your idea. I just made a few calls and now we're giving a party that will make a lot of kids happy and raise money for a won-derful cause." Nina closed her notebook and got up from the floor, where the three of them had pored over detail after detail for hours.

"Daddy is going to be so excited." Keisha smiled at Eric.

"I know I'm excited. It's on." Nina shouted.

"Like popcorn," Keisha and Eric finished together.

Chapter Thirty-four

Jade sat in Sean's lap in the chocolate and jade marble bath. She stretched her leg under the cascading water and let it splash in her face.

"Who picked out the colors for this bathroom?"

"I did." He gave her that smile that made her insides melt like butter.

"No, you didn't. You might have picked this wonderful brown, but your mother suggested the jade." She stood up and did a sensual dance.

"Come over here and do that." He pulled her toward him and she laughed.

"You didn't answer my question."

"What was the question?" He kissed his way up her leg to her thigh.

"I don't remember." She relaxed in his arms and sighed.

"I thought that might quiet you down."

They sat on the deck in bathrobes eating Belgian waffles with strawberries and whipped cream.

"These are wonderful, baby." She swirled a waffle through the cream and popped it in her mouth.

"My mom's secret recipe."

Jade continued eating without making a comment.

"Did I ever tell you I came to the museum that day because of my mother?"

"No." She waited to see what he would say next.

"I had just bought the house and we had spent time together doing renovations. She was just about to get on the plane back to Philly when she told me to buy some art for the walls. The next thing I know I was at the museum buying your art."

"I'm glad you listened to your mother." Jade smiled.

"I thought you were the most beautiful girl in the world with those pretty almond eyes."

"Really?" She looked surprised. "That's so sweet, Sean."

"I love all the dancing you've been doing. I would have loved to see you dance in some of those recitals at Spelman."

"I wished you had been there, too. But you get your own shows. You know I'm your private dancer." She smiled.

"Yeah, I liked that little stripper. Where did you learn how to do all of that stuff? My baby's got a little freak in her."

She doubled over laughing.

"I'll have to hire her again. Her prices were very reasonable."

"How come you never cook at the condo, Sean? I love it when you cook." She gathered the dishes and took them into the kitchen.

"That kitchen is too small. I can move around in this one."

She looked around the kitchen that spanned the width of the house. There was a breakfast area with a twenty-seven-inch color television built in the wall.

"It is a nice kitchen. And we've had some real good times up here."

"You like hanging out with me, don't you?" He was pulling her into his arms again. He wasn't able to keep his hands off of her and Jade loved it.

"I sure do. I love it. It feels like a vacation."

"It could be like this all the time. That's why I wanted you to stay home so we could spend time together and be like this."

"I'm sorry, baby. I must have been retarded. I'm not doing anything for at least a year so I can spend all my time with you and Kobe."

"After the concert you and I are taking ourselves a nice long vacation. We can leave Kobe with my mom. She'd love it."

"You've got yourself a date, Sean. I can't wait to go."

They were on their way upstairs when Jade spotted the mail on the table in the foyer. Dora, their housekeeper, had brought it in. Jade ripped open a large envelope and pulled out several copies of *Essence* with them on the cover. She was very pregnant and Sean was caressing her belly.

"When did we do this?" Sean picked up a copy of the magazine. "I forgot all about this photo shoot."

"I think it was in April. Nina made me do the interview. I felt like such a liar because we were having major problems then."

"It's a painting," he said. "But it looks just like a photograph."

"It's a little of both." She flipped open the magazine to a photo of the Santa Barbara house with Nina's byline.

"This is hot." He looked at Jade and grinned. "Let's go upstairs and read about Mr. and Mrs. Sylk Ross."

They cuddled up in the middle of the California King and took turns reading aloud from the magazine.

"At home with the Rosses . . . Jade Kimura says her biggest challenge has been adjusting her busy schedule to include time for her famous husband, their fifteen-month-old son, Kobe, and a burgeoning art career," Sean read.

"I had to learn everything as I went along. If it hadn't been for my sister friends, Keisha Johnson, wife of LA Laker small forward Eric Johnson; superstar singer Topaz; and Nina Beaubien, host of MTV's *Hollywood Hype*, I would never have made it. It also helps to have a patient, wonderful husband who loves me.

"That is so sweet, baby." Sean kissed her and continued reading. "Love is a gift, and when you find it, it's definitely worth fighting for, even dying for."

He finished the article and looked up at her. "I love you, baby, and I thank God for giving me the gift."

Chapter Thirty-five

Topaz sat in a guest bathroom that overlooked the Pacific at the ranch. It was the evening of the first annual Chocolate Affair. A stage had been set up down below where she would perform three songs to track with the ocean as her backdrop. TLC and Yolanda Adams were also on the show hosted by Chris Tucker.

It had been a crazy day that began with Eric's celebrity game at the Forum. His team ran Sean's off the floor. There were all sorts of NBA stars on both teams.

There was a pregame autograph party for the pediatric SCD patients and their families. Keisha pulled in the SCD Foundation and her Atlanta home girl, T-Boz, was the hostess. The kids had a chance to meet and take pictures with all their favorite celebrities.

Topaz ran a hand through her wet hair and poured herself a glass of champagne. *I have got to chill out.* She pulled a vial of cocaine out of her robe pocket and took several hits. She had purchased one to celebrate her marriage to Germain while trying to rid her mind of Sean and her baby. There was a knock at the door. It opened and Germain came in with a cup of tea.

"This is the first time I've ever been with my wife the diva."

She smiled and took a sip of the tea. "Thanks, baby."

"I'm so excited." He pulled her into his arms and kissed her. In a matter of seconds he had her burning with desire.

"Dang, baby. You always do this to me."

"So this is what goes on in the dressing room of a superstar." She was pulling down the zipper of his pants when there was a knock at the door.

"Damn." She put her robe back on when the knocking persisted. "No, this is what goes on in my dressing room. . . . What is it?"

Nina put a hand in her face, pushed the door open, and walked in. "Your hair . . ." She saw Germain leaning against the marble counter and stopped in her tracks. "Oh, my bad."

"Yeah, it was most definitely your bad timing." She had to smile at her cousin. "What do you want?"

"Your hairdresser is here." Nina smiled. "Hi, Germain. Bye, Germain." She walked out of the room and pulled the door up. "He'll be right up, so don't start anything you can't finish."

Topaz walked back into the room and smiled at Germain. "I guess you heard all that."

"The show must go on." He kissed her until she was breathless. "I'll be back," he said, mimicking Arnold Schwarzenegger. He could be just as big a ham as she could. Keisha always said they deserved each other.

She relaxed and rubbed some cocaine on her gums before Rudy came in. He wet her hair and twisted it into thick braids, adding in blond human hair. He fussed with her hair for an hour or so and had her looking like the Queen of Sheba. She gave him a gift bag with her CD and chocolate favors.

"Nina put these together. They're so cute." She held up the metallic gold bag with *Chocolate Affair* sprawled across it. "I signed the CD for you, babe." She kissed him and he was on his way. She was arranging her makeup on the antique dressing table when Keisha knocked and came in.

"I thought there was a lock on this door." Topaz walked over to the door and flipped the lock.

"No, you didn't." Keisha started laughing. "Who caught your little nasty behind up in here trying to get busy?"

Topaz burst into laughter and wiped the tears from her eyes. "You sure know how to ruin a sista's makeup. Speaking of makeup, I have a wedding album for you . . . and a CD. She reached into a suitcase and handed her a book of five-by-seven photos of everyone from the wedding.

"Oh, these are great." The two of them bent over the album admiring the photographs. "I was big, dang." She stood up and looked at herself in the mirror. Her curvy little waistline was back already and she was even more voluptuous. "You look great but that booty got bigger."

"And my man loves it. It's Eric's baby." She shimmied in the mirror.

"Now who's nasty?" Topaz began putting on her makeup. "You and Nina are just as bad, and then you try to blame everything on me."

"That's because you corrupted us. Miss Nina is deep. She was always ahead of her time. She schooled me on a lot of things when I came to LA." She thought of the white powder in her robe pocket.

"She's some kind of woman to get Kyle to marry her. No one else could and they did try."

"She corrupted him." She thought of the secret they shared.

"I hear Kyle's pretty good in that department, too. They're probably corrupting each other." Keisha laughed.

"All right. No more laughing, which means it's time for you to leave so I won't laugh anymore." She pulled on a pair of jeans and fastened a gold belt across her hips.

"I'm leaving, Topaz Lopez."

"What are you talking about?"

"That big juicy booty." Keisha laughed.

"What?" She looked in the mirror at her butt. "Hey." She started dancing the Tootsie Roll.

"You are one sick child. But thank you so much for doing the concert."

"Thank you for letting me. I'm honored. I love you, Key." She kissed her friend on the cheek.

"I love you, too. I'm so glad to see you smiling again. Germain makes you smile, girlfriend. You light up like a Christmas tree whenever he's around."

"That's because he lights me up."

"You are a nasty girl."

"And he loves it. But you know it's much more than that, Key."

"I know. That's why I'm so glad to see you together. You make him smile, too."

Topaz went into the bedroom and put on the rest of her clothing and jewelry. She had just slipped on a pair of sandals when there was a gentle knock at the door. She tapped across the room to open the door. Jade turned around and smiled.

She was exotically beautiful. The black hair, eyes, and her busy eyebrows against smooth caramel skin.

"You're ready. Good. I came up to escort the diva downstairs. TLC just went on."

"Do I look okay?" She looked at herself and turned around in front of the mirror.

"Yes. And I love your hair."

They chatted all the way downstairs to the library. There was a buffet set up and Topaz could look down at the concert. The ocean was a swirling black mass. Lights flickered across the horizon under a starry midnight sky.

"This is so beautiful," she whispered to herself.

"Wait, Baby Doll." Chris laughed as his little sister barreled into his mother.

"Turquoise." Topaz looked at Germain. "You guys have been playing rough again with my daughter."

"She's too much like you so we have to keep her in line."

A photographer came in and took pictures of the Gradneys.

"We're going back out and sit down. It's almost time for you to go on." He leaned in to kiss her.

"Here you go again. Just a little one now so I don't mess up my lipstick." He pulled gently on her bottom lip and left.

She had floated up into late summer night air with the music when Sean walked into the room.

"Did you see Jade? She told me she was coming up to escort you to the library."

"She did and I'm here." Topaz smiled.

Sean walked in and stood in front of her. "You look beautiful, as usual."

She smiled and wondered if he was thinking about the night they had made love. She sure was and his lips looked absolutely delicious.

"Thanks, Sean."

He bent down to kiss her on the cheek and she turned her face so their lips met. She couldn't wait for the touch of his on hers again, but he pushed her away.

"I was afraid this might happen." He found a handkerchief in his pocket and wiped his lips.

"What might happen?" For some reason she knew she wasn't going to like what he was going to say.

"You all over me."

"You arrogant bastard. Do you know who you're talking to?" She raised her hand to slap his face and he grabbed it.

"I know what you're acting like. Do you want your husband to walk in and see you behaving this way?"

She turned away from him and stood in front of the window.

"We both needed that night and now it's over. It should never have happened, but it did. I'm in love with my wife."

"I bet she can't make you feel the way I do." Her feelings were hurt and she was embarrassed by his rejection.

"You'd be surprised." He walked out of the room and she wanted to throw something at him.

"How dare he speak to me like that?" she huffed and puffed in front of the mirror. "The mother of his child. I should have told his ass about the baby, but I won't."

"What baby?" Keisha was there and then Jade walked in with Nina.

"Nothing." She looked at Jade and felt guilty and jealous all at once.

How could I do this to my friend?

"I need to duck in the bathroom for a second, ladies." She went into the bathroom and did the rest of the coke.

They led her outside to a packed house with standing room only. Nina had arranged for the concert to be taped and Hollywood's biggest and brightest were in attendance.

She saw Rosalyn coming toward her and looked for a way to avoid the woman.

"Topaz, there you are. Everything is so wonderful. I'm so glad I saw you."

Topaz kept walking toward the back of the stage.

"I've been looking for Turquoise." I wanted her to see my mother and father."

"Turquoise is with her father and brother. Neither you nor your mother and father will ever have anything to do with my daughter ever. Read the fine print on your contract. You sold those rights for three and a half million dollars."

Everyone cheered the moment she walked onto the stage. She greeted her audience and they cheered so much, she stood there and smiled and they cheered even louder.

"You all make me feel so special. But let's give a round of applause to the real stars tonight . . . the children."

She performed three songs, singing and dancing her heart out, and for a small amount of time, she forgot everyone and everything but the music.

Chapter Thirty-six

Nina hung up the telephone and danced. She ran around the living room screaming. Kyle, who was sitting there reading the financial section of the *New York Times*, slowly lowered the paper and peeped over the top of it at her.

"My gorgeous wife has blown a gasket, but I'm still gonna love her anyway," he sang, making up his own words to some old school jam.

"You are crazy." She plopped down next to him, her eyes sparkling with joy.

"What's up, girl? You can't hold out on a brother like that."

"Someone wants to buy my novel."

"I knew you'd sell it." He was just as excited as she was. "Simon and Schuster?"

"Yes. How did you know?"

"Because I prayed and because my baby got skills. You go, girl." They both got up and danced.

"Now I can retire so I can stay home and take care of you."

"Who's staying home? Nicki and I are going on the road with her daddy. I'll bring Rosa so we can always party. I was just looking at your schedule. I saw Hong Kong on there."

"And Tahiti and Greece and Paris." He tossed aside his paper.

"Those cities weren't on your schedule." Nina focused her dark brown eyes on her husband.

"That's true, but my new wife hasn't had the proper honeymoon yet."

"That's true, Mr. Ross, but every day with you is a honeymoon." She smiled and went to answer the phone. "The caterers are here, honey. Chop, chop."

"Is that ex-boyfriend of yours, Jamil, coming tonight with the rest of Hollywood?"

"Hollywood is not coming. Just a few friends." She opened the door and showed in the men who had arrived to set up for the luau.

"The house looks great, doesn't it, baby?" She smiled and looked around at the wallpaper, paint, and furniture that furnished their elegant Malibu estate.

"Yeah, it does now. Sean would never have stopped talking about us if we had let them in that night and they saw we didn't have any furniture."

She laughed and went for the phone. "That was your other brother and Karla at the gate."

A huge smile spread across his handsome face as he raced to the door to greet his identical twin brother.

"Check you out, man. You've gone Hollywood on us. I thought this was some rock star's house."

"Well, player, we always rocked and I am a star." Kyle laughed and hugged his brother.

Karla punched him in the arm. "You're a nut. That's what you are." They embraced and then she went to Nina.

"So how are you, Mrs. Ross, Miss I'm Never Gonna Get Married, Miss I'm Never Having a Baby? I never thought you would be the one to settle this wild man down."

Nina hugged her and smiled. "Stuff happens."

Karla folded her arms and looked at Kyle and Nina. "I saw you two at Kobe's dedication. I told Kirk something was up but he didn't want to believe it."

"Yeah, little brother. You really slipped a fast one on us."

Nina excused herself to go down to the beach to see how things were going for the housewarming. They were finally going to let everyone come over and see the house.

A small stage was up for the musicians and hula dancers. There was no roasted pig but there would be plenty of barbecued ribs, shrimp, and chicken for everyone. And there was a wonderful cake and plenty of Cristal. Since they never had a formal wedding they invited everyone over to celebrate. She looked around to make sure everything was in order.

"I have so many things to be thankful for. My wonderful husband, my healthy daughter, our beautiful home, and now my novel is going to be published."

She went back up to the house to get dressed. She looked outside and saw Kyle and Kirk on the beach with videocameras, and laughed. Sometimes she still couldn't believe she was married, and to Sean's brother.

The bedroom door opened and Kyle walked in with the camera and filmed Nina combing her hair. "After the concert, everybody kept saying you looked just like Chili from TLC. Do some TLC for me, baby." She picked up her hairbrush and started to sing and dance.

"Do that stuff, baby." He came in for a close-up and Nina stopped to laugh.

"Jade was right. You guys do act crazy when you all get together. "You better get dressed, Mr. Director."

"I've still got that footage." He laughed as he jumped in the shower.

She went downstairs and found that the rest of the gang had arrived.

"Dang, girl. Don't ever talk about me, Flash Gordon. This place is nice." Nina laughed and kissed Topaz and Germain, Chris and Turquoise.

"How's my pretty baby? My fat Turkey Lurkey." She took the little girl and lifted her in the air.

"My name is Baby Doll, Nina." She smiled and her amber eyes sparkled.

"Nina? I thought I was Ni-Ni, Miss Baby Doll. Who taught you how to speak so well?" Nina smiled at Chris, whose amber eyes sparkled up at her.

"Chris is such a little man." Keisha walked into the room and rubbed the little boy's head. "And he's such a good big brother."

"Germain is so wonderful with the children." Topaz looked at him with sparking amber eyes.

"Everyone will sure know these are your children, Topaz. They all have your eyes and mouth. Your mother spit all of you out." Keisha laughed.

Kyle came and took Nina by the hand. "They're ready to begin."

The Rosses and their immediate friends and family were seated right in front. A hush went over the party when the rhythms of the drums began. Jade was sitting beside Nina and she leaned over to whisper loudly in her ear.

"This is fabulous, Ni-Ni. My sister is the ultimate party planner."

Afterward, everyone went into the house to cut the cake on the terrace off of the dining room. Nina and Kyle stood in front of a gorgeous wedding cake with a cutter and sliced through the top layer. The group cheered as they fed each other cake.

Waiters poured flutes of sparkling juices and champagne. Sean stood up to make the toast.

"To my brother, Kyle, and his beautiful wife, Nina." He smiled and looked at everyone. "I never thought I'd use the word *wife* in a sentence with Kyle."

Kirk, Eric, and Germain laughed while Kyle made a face.

"I told you I was gonna get you back for what you did at my wedding, man." Sean looked at Eric and his brothers as they shared a private laugh together.

"Keep going, Sean. Kyle can't talk about anyone anymore." Jade laughed as she stood next to her husband and kissed him.

"Where was I?" Sean paused to collect his thoughts and the crowd exploded with fresh laughter.

"To my sister, Nina, and her wonderfully handsome husband who looks a lot like my boo. May you be eternally happy and blessed as you are today and always."

"Here, here." Sean clicked his glass to his wife's. "To our family and good friends, we love you always."

Nina looked around at her new family and her friends and smiled. It was still hard to believe sometimes that she was really married.

Marrying Jamil would have been the mistake of my life.

Kyle kissed her and everyone applauded. There was dancing on the marble floor in the dining room. A DJ supplied the latest and the greatest. Nina leaned back in Kyle's arms and looked up at him and sang along with Rufus and Chaka.

"All you need is an everlasting love."

He sang with her and they danced in the moonlight.

"I'm going to give you an everlasting love."

Postlude

Keisha ran upstairs to check on Rick after the cake had been cut. He was still asleep and Rosa was sitting next to Nicki's crib.

"Go downstairs and have some food. I'll sit with them for a while."

She patted Rick on the behind and looked in Nicki's crib. She was surprised to find the little girl awake, making a sound that resembled a hum and sucking on her hand.

"Hey, pretty Nicki." She lifted the child and smiled at her. She sat down in Rosa's rocker with the little girl in her arms.

"You are so precious." She gently kissed the baby on her forehead and smiled when Nicki looked up at her out of golden eyes. "Look at that baby's pretty eyes."

"Hey, girl. What are you doing?" Topaz stood in the doorway of the nursery.

"Just talking to Nicki. I believe she's trying to sing."

"She is? Oh, let me hold her." Topaz reached for the baby and Keisha placed her in her friend's arms.

"Can you sing, pretty baby? Can you sing?" She looked at the child and smiled.

231

"She has those golden eyes just like you."

"She does, doesn't she?" Topaz smiled. "You know Nina's mom and my mother are sisters."

"I know. Isn't it amazing how certain traits are passed on to one child and not to another?"

"Truly amazing." She sat in a chair and fussed over the baby.

Keisha watched her, smiling. Suddenly, she could hear Topaz's voice when they were children. *"I got my golden eyes from my daddy."*
Oh, my God.

Keisha's mind went back to Chris and Baby Doll, who had eyes like their mother. Her conversations with Eric and his suspicions of Topaz, and then she could hear Sean's voice.

"I should never have drunk that champagne."

Who loved champagne more than Topaz? The girl needed to own stock in Cristal. Keisha's head was spinning. Did Topaz really sleep with Sean as Eric had suggested?

She felt sick as all of the bits and pieces of the last year began falling into place . . . the sudden departure for Europe. Kyle's secret marriage to Nina and a baby. Nina never showing and not looking as though she had ever been pregnant.

Oh, my God . . . they're all part of it. That's why she showed up at the hospital crying all over the place.

Nina had taken her out of the room, and when Topaz returned, she was just there long enough to say good-bye to everyone and then she had left.

Nina appeared at the door with Jade.

"How's my beautiful niece?" Jade took the baby from Topaz and handed her to Nina.

Niece? Nicki is Topaz and Sean's love child.